Christmas Classics from the Modern Library

CHRISTMAS CLASSICS FROM THE MODERN LIBRARY

THE MODERN LIBRARY
NEW YORK

1997 Modern Library Edition

 Published in the United States by Random House, Inc., New York, and simultaneously in Canada by Random House of Canada Limited, Toronto.

Jacket illustration: *Holy Night*, after a painting by Karl Fuchs, courtesy of A.K.G., Berlin/SuperStock

LIBRARY OF CONGRESS CATALOGING-IN-PUBLICATION DATA
Christmas classics from the Modern Library.—1997 Modern Library ed.
p. cm.
ISBN 0-679-60282-8 (acid-free paper)
1. Christmas—Literary collections. I. Modern Library (Firm)
PN6071.C6C512 1997
808.8'0334—dc21 97-24012

Modern Library website address:
www.randomhouse.com/modernlibrary

Printed in the United States of America
on acid-free paper

2 4 6 8 9 7 5 3

A Note to the Reader

"Time was, with most of us, when Christmas Day, encircling all our limited world like a magic ring, left nothing out for us to miss or seek; bound together all our home enjoyments, affections and hopes; grouped everything and every one around the Christmas fire; and made the little picture shining in our bright young eyes, complete."

—*from* "What Christmas Is as We Grow Older" *by Charles Dickens*

What we now think of as the traditional Christmas celebration owes much to the vision of Charles Dickens. In his novels and stories, and especially in *A Christmas Carol,* Dickens established an ideal picture of the family gathering together to enjoy one another's company, to feast, and to make merry. It is in this spirit that the Modern Library offers its *Christmas Classics.* We hope that those of you who honor this season can find a moment to read aloud a couple of selections from our old Christmas favorites. You might want to recite a line or two of Donne or Milton, tell O. Henry's timeless fable or read the Christmas caper with Holmes and Watson; maybe even sing a carol or two—a few words to help to realize Dickens's idea of Christmas.

Season's greetings from the Modern Library!

Contents

The Bible Story

The story of Christ's birth is found in the Gospels of Matthew and Luke. It is presented here in the Authorized (King James) Version.

The Gospel According to Saint Matthew

CHAPTER 1

The book of the generation of Jesus Christ, the son of David, the
son of Abraham.
2 Abraham begat Isaac; and Isaac begat Jacob; and Jacob begat
Judas and his brethren;
3 And Judas begat Phares and Zara of Thamar; and Phares
begat Esrom; and Esrom begat Aram;
4 And Aram begat Aminadab; and Aminadab begat Naasson;
and Naasson begat Salmon;
5 And Salmon begat Booz of Rachab; and Booz begat Obed of
Ruth; and Obed begat Jesse;
6 And Jesse begat David the king; and David the king begat
Solomon of her *that had been the wife* of Urias;
7 And Solomon begat Roboam; and Roboam begat Abia; and
Abia begat Asa;

8 And Asa begat Josaphat; and Josaphat begat Joram; and Joram begat Ozias;

9 And Ozias begat Joatham; and Joatham begat Achaz; and Achaz begat Ezekias;

10 And Ezekias begat Manasses; and Manasses begat Amon; and Amon begat Josias;

11 And Josias begat Jechonias and his brethren, about the time they were carried away to Babylon:

12 And after they were brought to Babylon, Jechonias begat Salathiel; and Salathiel begat Zorobabel;

13 And Zorobabel begat Abiud; and Abiud begat Eliakim; and Eliakim begat Azor;

14 And Azor begat Sadoc; and Sadoc begat Achim; and Achim begat Eliud;

15 And Eliud begat Eleazar; and Eleazar begat Matthan; and Matthan begat Jacob;

16 And Jacob begat Joseph the husband of Mary, of whom was born Jesus, who is called Christ.

17 So all the generations from Abraham to David *are* fourteen generations; and from David until the carrying away into Babylon *are* fourteen generations; and from the carrying away into Babylon unto Christ *are* fourteen generations.

18 Now the birth of Jesus Christ was on this wise: When as his mother Mary was espoused to Joseph, before they came together, she was found with child of the Holy Ghost.

19 Then Joseph her husband, being a just *man*, and not willing to make her a publick example, was minded to put her away privily.

20 But while he thought on these things, behold, the angel of the Lord appeared unto him in a dream, saying, Joseph, thou son of

David, fear not to take unto thee Mary thy wife: for that which is
conceived in her is of the Holy Ghost.
21 And she shall bring forth a son, and thou shalt call his name
Jesus: for he shall save his people from their sins.
22 Now all this was done, that it might be fulfilled which was
spoken of the Lord by the prophet, saying,
23 Behold, a virgin shall be with child, and shall bring forth a
son, and they shall call his name Emmanuel, which being interpreted is, God with us.
24 Then Joseph being raised from sleep did as the angel of the
Lord had bidden him, and took unto him his wife:
25 And knew her not till she had brought forth her firstborn son:
and he called his name Jesus.

CHAPTER 2

Now when Jesus was born in Bethlehem of Judæa in the days of Herod the king, behold, there came wise men from the east to Jerusalem,
2 Saying, Where is he that is born King of the Jews? for we have
seen his star in the east, and are come to worship him.
3 When Herod the king had heard *these things*, he was troubled,
and all Jerusalem with him.
4 And when he had gathered all the chief priests and scribes of
the people together, he demanded of them where Christ should be born.
5 And they said unto him, In Bethlehem of Judæa: for thus it is
written by the prophet,

6 And thou Bethlehem, *in* the land of Juda, art not the least
among the princes of Juda: for out of thee shall come a Governor,
that shall rule my people Israel.
7 Then Herod, when he had privily called the wise men, in-
quired of them diligently what time the star appeared.
8 And he sent them to Bethlehem, and said, Go and search dili-
gently for the young child; and when ye have found *him,* bring me
word again, that I may come and worship him also.
9 When they had heard the king, they departed; and, lo, the star,
which they saw in the east, went before them, till it came and stood
over where the young child was.
10 When they saw the star, they rejoiced with exceeding great
joy.
11 And when they were come into the house, they saw the
young child with Mary his mother, and fell down, and worshipped
him: and when they had opened their treasures, they presented
unto him gifts; gold, and frankincense, and myrrh.
12 And being warned of God in a dream that they should not
return to Herod, they departed into their own country another way.
13 And when they were departed, behold, the angel of the Lord
appeareth to Joseph in a dream, saying, Arise, and take the young
child and his mother, and flee into Egypt, and be thou there until I
bring thee word: for Herod will seek the young child to destroy
him.
14 When he arose, he took the young child and his mother by
night, and departed into Egypt:
15 And was there until the death of Herod: that it might be ful-
filled which was spoken of the Lord by the prophet, saying, Out of
Egypt have I called my son.
16 Then Herod, when he saw that he was mocked of the wise

men, was exceeding wroth, and sent forth, and slew all the children
that were in Bethlehem, and in all the coasts thereof, from two
years old and under, according to the time which he had diligently
inquired of the wise men.

17 Then was fulfilled that which was spoken by Jeremy the
prophet, saying,

18 In Rama was there a voice heard, lamentation, and weeping,
and great mourning, Rachel weeping *for* her children, and would
not be comforted, because they are not.

19 But when Herod was dead, behold, an angel of the Lord ap-
peareth in a dream to Joseph in Egypt,

20 Saying, Arise, and take the young child and his mother, and
go into the land of Israel: for they are dead which sought the young
child's life.

21 And he arose, and took the young child and his mother, and
came into the land of Israel.

22 But when he heard that Archelaus did reign in Judæa in the
room of his father Herod, he was afraid to go thither: notwith-
standing, being warned of God in a dream, he turned aside into the
parts of Galilee:

23 And he came and dwelt in a city called Nazareth: that it
might be fulfilled which was spoken by the prophets, He shall be
called a Nazarene.

The Gospel According to Saint Luke

CHAPTER 1

Forasmuch as many have taken in hand to set forth in order a dec-
laration of those things which are most surely believed among us,
2 Even as they delivered them unto us, which from the begin-
ning were eyewitnesses, and ministers of the word;
3 It seemed good to me also, having had perfect understanding
of all things from the very first, to write unto thee in order, most ex-
cellent Theophilus,
4 That thou mightest know the certainty of those things,
wherein thou hast been instructed.
5 There was in the days of Herod, the king of Judæa, a certain
priest named Zacharias, of the course of Abia: and his wife *was* of
the daughters of Aaron, and her name *was* Elisabeth.
6 And they were both righteous before God, walking in all the
commandments and ordinances of the Lord blameless.

7 And they had no child, because that Elisabeth was barren, and
they both were *now* well stricken in years.
8 And it came to pass, that while he executed the priest's office
before God in the order of his course,
9 According to the custom of the priest's office, his lot was to
burn incense when he went into the temple of the Lord.
10 And the whole multitude of the people were praying with-
out at the time of incense.
11 And there appeared unto him an angel of the Lord standing
on the right side of the altar of incense.
12 And when Zacharias saw *him,* he was troubled, and fear fell
upon him.
13 But the angel said unto him, Fear not, Zacharias: for thy
prayer is heard; and thy wife Elisabeth shall bear thee a son, and
thou shalt call his name John.
14 And thou shalt have joy and gladness; and many shall rejoice
at his birth.
15 For he shall be great in the sight of the Lord, and shall drink
neither wine nor strong drink; and he shall be filled with the Holy
Ghost, even from his mother's womb.
16 And many of the children of Israel shall he turn to the Lord
their God.
17 And he shall go before him in the spirit and power of Elias, to
turn the hearts of the fathers to the children, and the disobedient to
the wisdom of the just; to make ready a people prepared for the Lord.
18 And Zacharias said unto the angel, Whereby shall I know
this? for I am an old man, and my wife well stricken in years.
19 And the angel answering said unto him, I am Gabriel, that
stand in the presence of God; and am sent to speak unto thee, and
to shew thee these glad tidings.

20 And, behold, thou shalt be dumb, and not able to speak, until the day that these things shall be performed, because thou believest not my words, which shall be fulfilled in their season.

21 And the people waited for Zacharias, and marvelled that he tarried so long in the temple.

22 And when he came out, he could not speak unto them: and they perceived that he had seen a vision in the temple: for he beckoned unto them, and remained speechless.

23 And it came to pass, that, as soon as the days of his ministration were accomplished, he departed to his own house.

24 And after those days his wife Elisabeth conceived, and hid herself five months, saying,

25 Thus hath the Lord dealt with me in the days wherein he looked on *me,* to take away my reproach among men.

26 And in the sixth month the angel Gabriel was sent from God unto a city of Galilee, named Nazareth,

27 To a virgin espoused to a man whose name was Joseph, of the house of David; and the virgin's name *was* Mary.

28 And the angel came in unto her, and said, Hail, *thou that art* highly favoured, the Lord *is* with thee: blessed *art* thou among women.

29 And when she saw *him,* she was troubled at his saying, and cast in her mind what manner of salutation this should be.

30 And the angel said unto her, Fear not, Mary: for thou hast found favour with God.

31 And, behold, thou shalt conceive in thy womb, and bring forth a son, and shalt call his name Jesus.

32 He shall be great, and shall be called the Son of the Highest: and the Lord God shall give unto him the throne of his father David:

33 And he shall reign over the house of Jacob for ever; and of his
kingdom there shall be no end.
34 Then said Mary unto the angel, How shall this be, seeing I
know not a man?
35 And the angel answered and said unto her, The Holy Ghost
shall come upon thee, and the power of the Highest shall over-
shadow thee: therefore also that holy thing which shall be born of
thee shall be called the Son of God.
36 And, behold, thy cousin Elisabeth, she hath also conceived a
son in her old age: and this is the sixth month with her, who was
called barren.
37 For with God nothing shall be impossible.
38 And Mary said, Behold the handmaid of the Lord; be it unto
me according to thy word. And the angel departed from her.
39 And Mary arose in those days, and went into the hill country
with haste, into a city of Juda;
40 And entered into the house of Zacharias, and saluted Elisa-
beth.
41 And it came to pass, that, when Elisabeth heard the saluta-
tion of Mary, the babe leaped in her womb; and Elisabeth was filled
with the Holy Ghost:
42 And she spake out with a loud voice, and said, Blessed *art*
thou among women, and blessed *is* the fruit of thy womb.
43 And whence *is* this to me, that the mother of my Lord should
come to me?
44 For, lo, as soon as the voice of thy salutation sounded in mine
ears, the babe leaped in my womb for joy.
45 And blessed *is* she that believed: for there shall be a perfor-
mance of those things which were told her from the Lord.
46 And Mary said, My soul doth magnify the Lord,

47 And my spirit hath rejoiced in God my Saviour.

48 For he hath regarded the low estate of his handmaiden: for, behold, from henceforth all generations shall call me blessed.

49 For he that is mighty hath done to me great things; and holy *is* his name.

50 And his mercy *is* on them that fear him from generation to generation.

51 He hath shewed strength with his arm; he hath scattered the proud in the imagination of their hearts.

52 He hath put down the mighty from *their* seats, and exalted them of low degree.

53 He hath filled the hungry with good things; and the rich he hath sent empty away.

54 He hath holpen his servant Israel, in remembrance of *his* mercy;

55 As he spake to our fathers, to Abraham, and to his seed for ever.

56 And Mary abode with her about three months, and returned to her own house.

57 Now Elisabeth's full time came that she should be delivered; and she brought forth a son.

58 And her neighbours and her cousins heard how the Lord had shewed great mercy upon her; and they rejoiced with her.

59 And it came to pass, that on the eighth day they came to circumcise the child; and they called him Zacharias, after the name of his father.

60 And his mother answered and said, Not *so;* but he shall be called John.

61 And they said unto her, There is none of thy kindred that is called by this name.

62 And they made signs to his father, how he would have him
called.

63 And he asked for a writing table, and wrote, saying, His name
is John. And they marvelled all.

64 And his mouth was opened immediately, and his tongue
loosed, and he spake, and praised God.

65 And fear came on all that dwelt round about them: and all
these sayings were noised abroad throughout all the hill country of
Judæa.

66 And all they that heard *them* laid *them* up in their hearts, say-
ing, What manner of child shall this be! And the hand of the Lord
was with him.

67 And his father Zacharias was filled with the Holy Ghost, and
prophesied, saying,

68 Blessed *be* the Lord God of Israel; for he hath visited and re-
deemed his people,

69 And hath raised up an horn of salvation for us in the house
of his servant David;

70 As he spake by the mouth of his holy prophets, which have
been since the world began:

71 That we should be saved from our enemies, and from the
hand of all that hate us;

72 To perform the mercy *promised* to our fathers, and to re-
member his holy covenant;

73 The oath which he sware to our father Abraham,

74 That he would grant unto us, that we being delivered out of
the hand of our enemies might serve him without fear,

75 In holiness and righteousness before him, all the days of our
life.

76 And thou, child, shalt be called the prophet of the Highest:
for thou shalt go before the face of the Lord to prepare his ways;
77 To give knowledge of salvation unto his people by the re-
mission of their sins,
78 Through the tender mercy of our God; whereby the day-
spring from on high hath visited us,
79 To give light to them that sit in darkness and *in* the shadow
of death, to guide our feet into the way of peace.
80 And the child grew, and waxed strong in spirit, and was in the
deserts till the day of his shewing unto Israel.

CHAPTER 2

And it came to pass in those days, that there went out a decree from
Cæsar Augustus, that all the world should be taxed.
2 (*And* this taxing was first made when Cyrenius was governor of
Syria.)
3 And all went to be taxed, every one into his own city.
4 And Joseph also went up from Galilee, out of the city of
Nazareth, into Judæa, unto the city of David, which is called Beth-
lehem; (because he was of the house and lineage of David:)
5 To be taxed with Mary his espoused wife, being great with
child.
6 And so it was, that, while they were there, the days were ac-
complished that she should be delivered.
7 And she brought forth her firstborn son, and wrapped him in
swaddling clothes, and laid him in a manger; because there was no
room for them in the inn.

8 And there were in the same country shepherds abiding in the field, keeping watch over their flock by night.

9 And, lo, the angel of the Lord came upon them, and the glory of the Lord shone round about them: and they were sore afraid.

10 And the angel said unto them, Fear not: for, behold, I bring you good tidings of great joy, which shall be to all people.

11 For unto you is born this day in the city of David a Saviour, which is Christ the Lord.

12 And this *shall* be a sign unto you; Ye shall find the babe wrapped in swaddling clothes, lying in a manger.

13 And suddenly there was with the angel a multitude of the heavenly host praising God, and saying,

14 Glory to God in the highest, and on earth peace, good will toward men.

15 And it came to pass, as the angels were gone away from them into heaven, the shepherds said one to another, Let us now go even unto Bethlehem, and see this thing which is come to pass, which the Lord hath made known unto us.

16 And they came with haste, and found Mary, and Joseph, and the babe lying in a manger.

17 And when they had seen *it*, they made known abroad the saying which was told them concerning this child.

18 And all they that heard *it* wondered at those things which were told them by the shepherds.

19 But Mary kept all these things, and pondered *them* in her heart.

20 And the shepherds returned, glorifying and praising God for all the things that they had heard and seen, as it was told unto them.

21 And when eight days were accomplished for the circumcis-

ing of the child, his name was called Jesus, which was so named of the angel before he was conceived in the womb.

22 And when the days of her purification according to the law of Moses were accomplished, they brought him to Jerusalem, to present *him* to the Lord;

23 (As it is written in the law of the Lord, Every male that openeth the womb shall be called holy to the Lord;)

24 And to offer a sacrifice according to that which is said in the law of the Lord, A pair of turtledoves, or two young pigeons.

25 And, behold, there was a man in Jerusalem, whose name *was* Simeon; and the same man *was* just and devout, waiting for the consolation of Israel: and the Holy Ghost was upon him.

26 And it was revealed unto him by the Holy Ghost, that he should not see death, before he had seen the Lord's Christ.

27 And he came by the Spirit into the temple: and when the parents brought in the child Jesus, to do for him after the custom of the law,

28 Then took he him up in his arms, and blessed God, and said,

29 Lord, now lettest thou thy servant depart in peace, according to thy word:

30 For mine eyes have seen thy salvation,

31 Which thou hast prepared before the face of all people;

32 A light to lighten the Gentiles, and the glory of thy people Israel.

33 And Joseph and his mother marvelled at those things which were spoken of him.

34 And Simeon blessed them, and said unto Mary his mother, Behold, this *child* is set for the fall and rising again of many in Israel; and for a sign which shall be spoken against;

35 (Yea, a sword shall pierce through thy own soul also,) that the thoughts of many hearts may be revealed.

36 And there was one Anna, a prophetess, the daughter of Phanuel, of the tribe of Aser: she was of a great age, and had lived with an husband seven years from her virginity;

37 And she *was* a widow of about fourscore and four years, which departed not from the temple, but served *God* with fastings and prayers night and day.

38 And she coming in that instant gave thanks likewise unto the Lord, and spake of him to all them that looked for redemption in Jerusalem.

39 And when they had performed all things according to the law of the Lord, they returned into Galilee, to their own city Nazareth.

40 And the child grew, and waxed strong in spirit, filled with wisdom: and the grace of God was upon him.

41 Now his parents went to Jerusalem every year at the feast of the passover.

42 And when he was twelve years old, they went up to Jerusalem after the custom of the feast.

43 And when they had fulfilled the days, as they returned, the child Jesus tarried behind in Jerusalem; and Joseph and his mother knew not *of it.*

44 But they, supposing him to have been in the company, went a day's journey; and they sought him among *their* kinsfolk and acquaintance.

45 And when they found him not, they turned back again to Jerusalem, seeking him.

46 And it came to pass, that after three days they found him in the temple, sitting in the midst of the doctors, both hearing them, and asking them questions.

47 And all that heard him were astonished at his understanding and answers.

48 And when they saw him, they were amazed: and his mother said unto him, Son, why hast thou thus dealt with us? behold, thy father and I have sought thee sorrowing.

49 And he said unto them, How is it that ye sought me? wist ye not that I must be about my Father's business?

50 And they understood not the saying which he spake unto them.

51 And he went down with them, and came to Nazareth, and was subject unto them: but his mother kept all these sayings in her heart.

52 And Jesus increased in wisdom and stature, and in favour with God and man.

EXCERPTS

The best known of all Christmas stories is Charles Dickens's A Christmas Carol. *Since its publication in 1843, the story of Ebenezer Scrooge's transformation has come to represent the very essence of the season. Here, Scrooge is confronted by the Ghost of Christmas Yet To Come and visits the home of Bob Cratchit, his downtrodden clerk.*

"Playing Pilgrims" and "A Merry Christmas" were published in the first part of Little Women *in 1868. Louisa May Alcott had hitherto published pseudonymous thrillers to supplement her family's meager income. In* Little Women, *she drew upon her childhood experiences, wrote herself into Jo March, and created one of the most lively and beloved families in all fiction.*

The Pickwick Papers *was published in serial form between 1836 and 1837. In this brief extract, Mr. Pickwick assembles a Christmas expedition.*

From
A Christmas Carol

STAVE IV

The Last of the Spirits

The Phantom slowly, gravely, silently, approached. When it came near him, Scrooge bent down upon his knee; for in the very air through which this Spirit moved it seemed to scatter gloom and mystery.

It was shrouded in a deep black garment, which concealed its head, its face, its form, and left nothing of it visible save one outstretched hand. But for this it would have been difficult to detach its figure from the night, and separate it from the darkness by which it was surrounded.

He felt that it was tall and stately when it came beside him, and that its mysterious presence filled him with a solemn dread. He knew no more, for the Spirit neither spoke nor moved.

"I am in the presence of the Ghost of Christmas Yet To Come?" said Scrooge.

The Spirit answered not, but pointed onward with its hand.

"You are about to show me shadows of the things that have not happened, but will happen in the time before us," Scrooge pursued. "Is that so, Spirit?"

The upper portion of the garment was contracted for an instant in its folds, as if the Spirit had inclined its head. That was the only answer he received.

Although well used to ghostly company by this time, Scrooge feared the silent shape so much that his legs trembled beneath him, and he found that he could hardly stand when he prepared to follow it. The Spirit paused a moment, as observing his condition, and giving him time to recover.

But Scrooge was all the worse for this. It thrilled him with a vague uncertain horror, to know that behind the dusky shroud, there were ghostly eyes intently fixed upon him, while he, though he stretched his own to the utmost, could see nothing but a spectral hand and one great heap of black.

"Ghost of the Future!" he exclaimed, "I fear you more than any Spectre I have seen. But as I know your purpose is to do me good, and as I hope to live to be another man from what I was, I am prepared to bear you company, and do it with a thankful heart. Will you not speak to me?"

It gave him no reply. The hand was pointed straight before them.

"Lead on!" said Scrooge. "Lead on! The night is waning fast, and it is precious time to me, I know. Lead on, Spirit!"

The Phantom moved away as it had come towards him. Scrooge followed in the shadow of its dress, which bore him up, he thought, and carried him along.

They scarcely seemed to enter the city; for the city rather seemed to spring up about them, and encompass them of its own act. But there they were, in the heart of it; on 'Change, amongst the merchants; who hurried up and down, and chinked the money in their pockets, and conversed in groups, and looked at their watches, and trifled thoughtfully with their great gold seals; and so forth, as Scrooge had seen them often.

The Spirit stopped beside one little knot of business men. Observing that the hand was pointed to them, Scrooge advanced to listen to their talk.

"No," said a great fat man with a monstrous chin, "I don't know much about it, either way. I only know he's dead."

"When did he die?" inquired another.

"Last night, I believe."

"Why, what was the matter with him?" asked a third, taking a vast quantity of snuff out of a very large snuff-box. "I thought he'd never die."

"God knows," said the first, with a yawn.

"What has he done with his money?" asked a red-faced gentleman with a pendulous excrescence on the end of his nose, that shook like the gills of a turkey-cock.

"I haven't heard," said the man with the large chin, yawning again. "Left it to his Company, perhaps. He hasn't left it to *me.* That's all I know."

This pleasantry was received with a general laugh.

"It's likely to be a very cheap funeral," said the same speaker; "for upon my life I don't know of anybody to go to it. Suppose we make up a party and volunteer?"

"I don't mind going if a lunch is provided," observed the gentleman with the excrescence on his nose. "But I must be fed, if I make one."

Another laugh.

"Well, I am the most disinterested among you, after all," said the first speaker, "for I never wear black gloves, and I never eat lunch.

But I'll offer to go, if anybody else will. When I come to think of it, I'm not at all sure that I wasn't his most particular friend; for we used to stop and speak whenever we met. Bye, bye!"

Speakers and listeners strolled away, and mixed with other groups. Scrooge knew the men, and looked towards the Spirit for an explanation.

The Phantom glided on into a street. Its finger pointed to two persons meeting. Scrooge listened again, thinking that the explanation might lie here.

He knew these men, also, perfectly. They were men of business: very wealthy, and of great importance. He had made a point always of standing well in their esteem: in a business point of view, that is; strictly in a business point of view.

"How are you?" said one.

"How are you?" returned the other.

"Well!" said the first. "Old Scratch has got his own at last, hey?"

"So I am told," returned the second. "Cold, isn't it?"

"Seasonable for Christmas time. You're not a skaiter, I suppose?"

"No. No. Something else to think of. Good morning!"

Not another word. That was their meeting, their conversation, and their parting.

Scrooge was at first inclined to be surprised that the Spirit should attach importance to conversations apparently so trivial; but feeling assured that they must have some hidden purpose, he set himself to consider what it was likely to be. They could scarcely be supposed to have any bearing on the death of Jacob, his old partner, for that was Past, and this Ghost's province was the Future. Nor could he think of any one immediately connected with himself, to whom he could apply them. But nothing doubting that to whomsoever they applied they had some latent moral for his own improvement, he resolved to treasure up every word he heard, and everything he saw; and especially to observe the shadow of himself when it appeared. For he had an expectation that the conduct of his future self would give him the clue he missed, and would render the solution of these riddles easy.

He looked about in that very place for his own image; but another man stood in his accustomed corner, and though the clock pointed to his usual time of day for being there, he saw no likeness of himself among the multitudes that poured in through the Porch. It gave him little surprise, however; for he had been revolving in his mind a change of life, and thought and hoped he saw his new-born resolutions carried out in this.

Quiet and dark, beside him stood the Phantom, with its outstretched hand. When he roused himself from his thoughtful quest, he fancied from the turn of the hand, and its situation in reference to himself, that the Unseen Eyes were looking at him keenly. It made him shudder, and feel very cold.

They left the busy scene, and went into an obscure part of the town, where Scrooge had never penetrated before although he recognised its situation, and its bad repute. The ways were foul and narrow; the shops and houses wretched; the people half-naked, drunken, slipshod, ugly. Alleys and archways, like so many cesspools, disgorged their offences of smell, and dirt, and life, upon the straggling streets; and the whole quarter reeked with crime, with filth, and misery.

Far in this den of infamous resort, there was a low-browed, beetling shop, below a pent-house roof, where iron, old rags, bottles, bones, and greasy offal, were bought. Upon the floor within, were piled up heaps of rusty keys, nails, chains, hinges, files, scales, weights, and refuse iron of all kinds. Secrets that few would like to scrutinise were bred and hidden in mountains of unseemly rags, masses of corrupted fat, and sepulchres of bones. Sitting in among the wares he dealt in, by a charcoal-stove, made of old bricks, was a gray-haired rascal, nearly seventy years of age; who had screened himself from the cold air without, by a frousy curtaining of miscellaneous tatters, hung upon a line; and smoked his pipe in all the luxury of calm retirement.

Scrooge and the Phantom came into the presence of this man, just as a woman with a heavy bundle slunk into the shop. But she had scarcely entered, when another woman, similarly laden, came in too; and she was closely followed by a man in faded black, who was no less startled by the sight of them, than they had been upon the recognition of each other. After a short period of blank astonishment, in which the old man with the pipe had joined them, they all three burst into a laugh.

"Let the charwoman alone to be the first!" cried she who had entered first. "Let the laundress alone to be the second; and let the undertaker's man alone to be the third. Look here, old Joe, here's a chance! If we haven't all three met here without meaning it."

"You couldn't have met in a better place," said old Joe, removing his pipe from his mouth. "Come into the parlour. You were made free of it long ago, you know; and the other two an't strangers. Stop till I shut the door of the shop. Ah! How it skreeks! There an't such a rusty bit of metal in the place as its own hinges, I believe; and I'm sure there's no such old bones here, as mine. Ha, ha! We're all suitable to our calling, we're well matched. Come into the parlour. Come into the parlour."

The parlour was the space behind the screen of rags. The old man raked the fire together with an old stair-rod, and having trimmed his smoky lamp (for it was night), with the stem of his pipe, put it in his mouth again.

While he did this, the woman who had already spoken threw her bundle on the floor and sat down in a flaunting manner on a stool; crossing her elbows on her knees, and looking with a bold defiance at the other two.

"What odds then! What odds, Mrs. Dilber?" said the woman. "Every person has a right to take care of themselves. *He* always did!"

"That's true, indeed!" said the laundress. "No man more so."

"Why then, don't stand staring as if you was afraid, woman; who's the wiser? We're not going to pick holes in each other's coats, I suppose?"

"No, indeed!" said Mrs. Dilber and the man together. "We should hope not."

"Very well, then!" cried the woman. "That's enough. Who's the worse for the loss of a few things like these? Not a dead man, I suppose."

"No, indeed," said Mrs. Dilber, laughing.

"If he wanted to keep 'em after he was dead, a wicked old screw," pursued the women, "why wasn't he natural in his lifetime? If he had been, he'd have had somebody to look after him when he was struck with Death, instead of lying gasping out his last there, alone by himself."

"It's the truest word that ever was spoke," said Mrs. Dilber. "It's a judgment on him."

"I wish it was a little heavier one," replied the woman; "and it should have been, you may depend upon it, if I could have laid my hands on anything else. Open that bundle, old Joe, and let me know the value of it. Speak out plain. I'm not afraid to be the first, nor afraid for them to see it. We knew pretty well that we were helping ourselves, before we met here, I believe. It's no sin. Open the bundle, Joe."

But the gallantry of her friends would not allow of this; and the man in faded black, mounting the breach first, produced *his* plunder. It was not extensive. A seal or two, a pencil-case, a pair of sleeve-buttons, and a brooch of no great value, were all. They were severally examined and appraised by old Joe, who chalked the sums he was disposed to give for each, upon the wall, and added them up into a total when he found there was nothing more to come.

"That's your account," said Joe, "and I wouldn't give another sixpence, if I was to be boiled for not doing it. Who's next?"

Mrs. Dilber was next. Sheets and towels, a little wearing apparel, two old-fashioned silver teaspoons, a pair of sugartongs, and a few boots. Her account was stated on the wall in the same manner.

"I always give too much to ladies. It's a weakness of mine, and that's the way I ruin myself," said old Joe. "That's your account. If you asked me for another penny, and made it an open question, I'd repent of being so liberal and knock off half-a-crown."

"And now undo *my* bundle, Joe," said the first woman.

Joe went down on his knees for the greater convenience of opening it, and having unfastened a great many knots, dragged out a large and heavy roll of some dark stuff.

"What do you call this?" said Joe. "Bed-curtains!"

"Ah!" returned the woman, laughing and leaning forward on her crossed arms. "Bed-curtains!"

"You don't mean to say you took 'em down, rings and all, with him lying there?" said Joe.

"Yes I do," replied the woman. "Why not?"

"You were born to make your fortune," said Joe, "and you'll certainly do it."

"I certainly shan't hold my hand, when I get anything in it by reaching it out, for the sake of such a man as He was, I promise you, Joe," returned the woman coolly. "Don't drop that oil upon the blankets, now."

"His blankets?" asked Joe.

"Whose else's do you think?" replied the woman. "He isn't likely to take cold without 'em, I dare say."

"I hope he didn't die of anything catching? Eh?" said old Joe, stopping in his work, and looking up.

"Don't you be afraid of that," returned the woman. "I an't so fond of his company that I'd loiter about him for such things, if he did. Ah! you may look through that shirt till your eyes ache; but you won't find a hole in it, nor a thread-bare place. It's the best he had, and a fine one too. They'd have wasted it, if it hadn't been for me."

"What do you call wasting of it?" asked old Joe.

"Putting it on him to be buried in, to be sure," replied the woman with a laugh. "Somebody was fool enough to do it, but I took it off again. If calico an't good enough for such a purpose, it isn't good enough for anything. It's quite as becoming to the body. He can't look uglier than he did in that one."

Scrooge listened to this dialogue in horror. As they sat grouped about their spoil, in the scanty light afforded by the old man's lamp, he viewed them with a detestation and disgust, which could hardly have been greater, though they had been obscene demons, marketing the corpse itself.

"He, ha!" laughed the same woman, when old Joe, producing a flannel bag with money in it, told out their several gains upon the ground. "This is the end of it, you see! He frightened every one away from him when he was alive, to profit us when he was dead! Ha, ha, ha!"

"Spirit!" said Scrooge, shuddering from head to foot. "I see, I see. The case of this unhappy man might be my own. My life tends that way, now. Merciful Heaven, what is this!"

He recoiled in terror, for the scene had changed, and now he almost touched a bed: a bare, uncurtained bed: on which, beneath a ragged sheet, there lay a something covered up, which, though it was dumb, announced itself in awful language.

The room was very dark, too dark to be observed with any accuracy, though Scrooge glanced round it in obedience to a secret impulse, anxious to know what kind of room it was. A pale light, rising in the outer air, fell straight upon the bed; and on it, plundered and bereft, unwatched, unwept, uncared for, was the body of this man.

Scrooge glanced towards the Phantom. Its steady hand was pointed to the head. The cover was so carelessly adjusted that the slightest raising of it, the motion of a finger upon Scrooge's part, would have disclosed the face. He thought of it, felt how easy it would be to do, and longed to do it; but had no more power to withdraw the veil than to dismiss the spectre at his side.

Oh cold, cold, rigid, dreadful Death, set up thine altar here, and dress it with such terrors as thou hast at thy command: for this is thy dominion! But of the loved, revered, and honoured head, thou canst not turn one hair to thy dread purposes, or make one feature odious. It is not that the hand is heavy and will fall down when released; it is not that the heart and pulse are still; but that the hand WAS open, generous, and true; the heart brave, warm, and tender; and the pulse a man's. Strike, Shadow, strike! And see his good deeds springing from the wound, to sow the world with life immortal!

No voice pronounced these words in Scrooge's ears, and yet he heard them when he looked upon the bed. He thought, if this man could be raised up now, what would be his foremost thoughts? Avarice, hard dealing, griping cares? They have brought him to a rich end, truly!

He lay, in the dark empty house, with not a man, a woman, or a child, to say that he was kind to me in this or that, and for the memory of one kind word I will be kind to him. A cat was tearing at the door, and there was a sound of gnawing rats beneath the hearth-stone. What *they* wanted in the room of death, and why they were so restless and disturbed, Scrooge did not dare to think.

"Spirit!" he said, "this is a fearful place. In leaving it, I shall not leave its lesson, trust me. Let us go!"

Still the Ghost pointed with an unmoved finger to the head.

"I understand you," Scrooge returned, "and I would do it, if I could. But I have not the power, Spirit. I have not the power."

Again it seemed to look upon him.

"If there is any person in the town, who feels emotion caused by this man's death," said Scrooge quite agonised, "show that person to me, Spirit, I beseech you!"

The Phantom spread its dark robe before him for a moment, like a wing; and withdrawing it, revealed a room by daylight, where a mother and her children were.

She was expecting some one, and with anxious eagerness; for she walked up and down the room; started at every sound; looked out from the window; glanced at the clock; tried, but in vain, to work with her needle; and could hardly bear the voices of the children in their play.

At length the long-expected knock was heard. She hurried to the door, and met her husband; a man whose face was care-worn and depressed, though he was young. There was a remarkable expression in it now; a kind of serious delight of which he felt ashamed, and which he struggled to repress.

He sat down to the dinner that had been hoarding for him by the fire; and when she asked him faintly what news (which was not until after a long silence), he appeared embarrassed how to answer.

"Is it good," she said, "or bad?"—to help him.

"Bad," he answered.

"We are quite ruined?"

"No. There is hope yet, Caroline."

"If *he* relents," she said, amazed, "there is! Nothing is past hope, if such a miracle has happened."

"He is past relenting," said her husband. "He is dead."

She was a mild and patient creature if her face spoke truth; but she was thankful in her soul to hear it, and she said so, with clasped hands. She prayed forgiveness the next moment, and was sorry; but the first was the emotion of her heart.

"What the half-drunken woman whom I told you of last night, said to me, when I tried to see him and obtain a week's delay; and what I thought was a mere excuse to avoid me; turns out to have been quite true. He was not only very ill, but dying, then."

"To whom will our debt be transferred?"

"I don't know. But before that time we shall be ready with the money; and even though we were not, it would be bad fortune indeed to find so merciless a creditor in his successor. We may sleep to-night with light hearts, Caroline!"

Yes. Soften it as they would, their hearts were lighter. The children's faces, hushed and clustered round to hear what they so little understood, were brighter; and it was a happier house for this man's death! The only emotion that the Ghost could show him, caused by the event, was one of pleasure.

"Let me see some tenderness connected with a death," said Scrooge; "or that dark chamber, Spirit, which we left just now, will be for ever present to me."

The Ghost conducted him through several streets familiar to his feet; and as they went along, Scrooge looked here and there to find himself, but nowhere was he to be seen. They entered poor Bob Cratchit's house; the dwelling he had visited before; and found the mother and the children seated round the fire.

Quiet. Very quiet. The noisy little Cratchits were as still as statues in one corner, and sat looking up at Peter, who had a book before him. The mother and her daughters were engaged in sewing. But surely they were very quiet!

" 'And He took a child, and set him in the midst of them.' "

Where had Scrooge heard those words? He had not dreamed them. The boy must have read them out, as he and the Spirit crossed the threshold. Why did he not go on?

The mother laid her work upon the table, and put her hand up to her face.

"The colour hurts my eyes," she said.

The colour? Ah, poor Tiny Tim!

"They're better now again," said Cratchit's wife. "It makes them weak by candle-light; and I wouldn't show weak eyes to your father when he comes home, for the world. It must be near his time."

"Past it rather," Peter answered, shutting up his book. "But I think he's walked a little slower than he used, these few last evenings, mother."

They were very quiet again. At last she said, and in a steady, cheerful voice, that only faultered once:

"I have known him walk with—I have known him walk with Tiny Tim upon his shoulder, very fast indeed."

"And so have I," cried Peter. "Often."

"And so have I!" exclaimed another. So had all.

"But he was very light to carry," she resumed, intent upon her work, "and his father loved him so, that it was no trouble—no trouble. And there is your father at the door!"

She hurried out to meet him; and little Bob in his comforter—he had need of it, poor fellow—came in. His tea was ready for him on the hob, and they all tried who should help him to it most. Then the two young Cratchits got upon his knees and laid, each child a little cheek, against his face, as if they said, "Don't mind it, father. Don't be grieved!"

Bob was very cheerful with them, and spoke pleasantly to all the family. He looked at the work upon the table, and praised the industry and speed of Mrs. Cratchit and the girls. They would be done long before Sunday, he said.

"Sunday! You went to-day then, Robert?" said his wife.

"Yes, my dear," returned Bob. "I wish you could have gone. It would have done you good to see how green a place it is. But you'll see it often. I promised him that I would walk there on a Sunday. My little, little child!" cried Bob. "My little child!"

He broke down all at once. He couldn't help it. If he could have helped it, he and his child would have been farther apart perhaps than they were.

He left the room, and went up stairs into the room above, which was lighted cheerfully, and hung with Christmas. There was a chair set close beside the child, and there were signs of some one having been there, lately. Poor Bob sat down in it, and when he had thought a little and composed himself, he kissed the little face. He was reconciled to what had happened, and went down again quite happy.

They drew about the fire, and talked; the girls and mother working still. Bob told them of the extraordinary kindness of Mr. Scrooge's nephew, whom he had scarcely seen but once, and who, meeting him in the street that day, and seeing that he looked a little—"just a little down you know" said Bob, inquired what had happened to distress him. "On which," said Bob, "for he is the pleasantest-spoken gentleman you ever heard, I told him. 'I am heartily sorry for it, Mr. Cratchit,' he said, 'and heartily sorry for your good wife.' By the bye, how he ever knew *that,* I don't know."

"Knew what, my dear?"

"Why, that you were a good wife," replied Bob.

"Everybody knows that!" said Peter.

"Very well observed, my boy!" cried Bob. "I hope they do. 'Heartily sorry,' he said, 'for your good wife. If I can be of service to you in any way,' he said, giving me his card, 'that's where I live. Pray come to me.' Now, it wasn't," cried Bob, "for the sake of anything he might be able to do for us, so much as for his kind way, that this was quite delightful. It really seemed as if he had known our Tiny Tim, and felt with us."

"I'm sure he's a good soul!" said Mrs. Cratchit.

"You would be sure of it, my dear," returned Bob, "if you saw and spoke to him. I shouldn't be at all surprised, mark what I say, if he got Peter a better situation."

"Only hear that, Peter," said Mrs. Cratchit.

"And then," cried one of the girls, "Peter will be keeping company with some one, and setting up for himself."

"Get along with you!" retorted Peter, grinning.

"It's just as likely as not," said Bob, "one of these days; though there's plenty of time for that, my dear. But however and whenever we part from one another, I am sure we shall none of us forget poor Tiny Tim—shall we—or this first parting that there was among us?"

"Never, father!" cried they all.

"And I know," said Bob, "I know, my dears, that when we recollect how patient and how mild he was; although he was a little, little child; we shall not quarrel easily among ourselves, and forget poor Tiny Tim in doing it."

"No, never, father!" they all cried again.

"I am very happy," said little Bob, "I am very happy!"

Mrs. Cratchit kissed him, his daughters kissed him, the two young Cratchits kissed him, and Peter and himself shook hands. Spirit of Tiny Tim, thy childish essence was from God!

"Spectre," said Scrooge, "something informs me that our parting moment is at hand. I know it, but I know not how. Tell me what man that was whom we saw lying dead?"

The Ghost of Christmas Yet To Come conveyed him, as before—though at a different time, he thought: indeed, there seemed no order in these latter visions, save that they were in the Future—into the resorts of business men, but showed him not himself. Indeed, the Spirit did not stay for anything, but went straight on, as to the end just now desired, until besought by Scrooge to tarry for a moment.

"This court," said Scrooge, "through which we hurry now, is where my place of occupation is, and has been for a length of time. I see the house. Let me behold what I shall be, in days to come."

The Spirit stopped; the hand was pointed elsewhere.

"The house is yonder," Scrooge exclaimed. "Why do you point away?"

The inexorable finger underwent no change.

Scrooge hastened to the window of his office, and looked in. It was an office still, but not his. The furniture was not the same, and the figure in the chair was not himself. The Phantom pointed as before.

He joined it once again, and wondering why and whither he had gone, accompanied it until they reached an iron gate. He paused to look round before entering.

A churchyard. Here, then, the wretched man whose name he had now to learn, lay underneath the ground. It was a worthy place. Walled in by houses; overrun by grass and weeds, the growth of vegetation's death, not life; choked up with too much burying; fat with repleted appetite. A worthy place!

The Spirit stood among the graves, and pointed down to One. He advanced towards it trembling. The Phantom was exactly as it had been, but he dreaded that he saw new meaning in its solemn shape.

"Before I draw nearer to that stone to which you point," said Scrooge, "answer me one question. Are these the shadows of the things that Will be, or are they shadows of things that May be, only?"

Still the Ghost pointed downward to the grave by which it stood.

"Men's courses will foreshadow certain ends, to which, if persevered in, they must lead," said Scrooge. "But if the courses be departed from, the ends will change. Say it is thus with what you show me!"

The Spirit was immovable as ever.

Scrooge crept towards it, trembling as he went; and following the finger, read upon the stone of the neglected grave his own name, EBENEZER SCROOGE.

"Am *I* that man who lay upon the bed?" he cried, upon his knees.

The finger pointed from the grave to him, and back again.

"No, Spirit! Oh, no, no!"

The finger still was there.

"Spirit!" he cried, tight clutching at its robe, "hear me! I am not the man I was. I will not be the man I must have been but for this intercourse. Why show me this, if I am past all hope?"

For the first time the hand appeared to shake.

"Good Spirit," he pursued, as down upon the ground he fell before it: "Your nature intercedes for me, and pities me. Assure me that I yet may change these shadows you have shown me, by an altered life!"

The kind hand trembled.

"I will honour Christmas in my heart, and try to keep it all the year. I will live in the Past, the Present, and the Future. The Spirits of all Three shall strive within me. I will not shut out the lessons that they teach. Oh, tell me I may sponge away the writing on this stone!"

In his agony, he caught the spectral hand. It sought to free itself, but he was strong in his entreaty, and detained it. The Spirit, stronger yet, repulsed him.

Holding up his hands in a last prayer to have his fate reversed, he saw an alteration in the Phantom's hood and dress. It shrunk, collapsed, and dwindled down into a bedpost.

From

Little Women

CHAPTER 1

Playing Pilgrims

"Christmas won't be Christmas without any presents," grumbled Jo, lying on the rug.

"It's so dreadful to be poor!" sighed Meg, looking down at her old dress.

"I don't think it's fair for some girls to have plenty of pretty things, and other girls nothing at all," added little Amy, with an injured sniff.

"We've got Father and Mother and each other," said Beth contentedly from her corner.

The four young faces on which the firelight shone brightened at the cheerful words, but darkened again as Jo said sadly, "We haven't got Father, and shall not have him for a long time." She didn't say "perhaps never," but each silently added it, thinking of Father far away, where the fighting was.

Nobody spoke for a minute; then Meg said in an altered tone, "You know the reason Mother proposed not having any presents this Christmas was because it is going to be a hard winter for everyone; and she thinks we ought not to spend money for pleasure, when our men are suffering so in the army. We can't do much, but we can make our little sacrifices, and ought to do it gladly. But I am afraid I don't." And Meg shook her head, as she thought regretfully of all the pretty things she wanted.

"But I don't think the little we should spend would do any good. We've each got a dollar, and the army wouldn't be much helped by our giving that. I agree not to expect anything from Mother or you, but I do want to buy *Undine and Sintram* for myself. I've wanted it *so* long," said Jo, who was a bookworm.

"I planned to spend mine in new music," said Beth, with a little sigh, which no one heard but the hearth brush and kettle holder.

"I shall get a nice box of Faber's drawing pencils. I really need them," said Amy decidedly.

"Mother didn't say anything about our money, and she won't wish us to give up everything. Let's each buy what we want, and have a little fun. I'm sure we work hard enough to earn it," cried Jo, examining the heels of her shoes in a gentlemanly manner.

"I know *I* do—teaching those tiresome children nearly all day, when I'm longing to enjoy myself at home," began Meg, in the complaining tone again.

"You don't have half such a hard time as I do," said Jo. "How would you like to be shut up for hours with a nervous, fussy old lady, who keeps you trotting, is never satisfied, and worries you till you're ready to fly out of the window or cry?"

"It's naughty to fret, but I do think washing dishes and keeping things tidy is the worst work in the world. It makes me cross, and my hands get so stiff, I can't practice well at all." And Beth looked at her rough hands with a sigh that any one could hear that time.

"I don't believe any of you suffer as I do," cried Amy, "for you don't have to go to school with impertinent girls, who plague you if you don't know your lessons, and laugh at your dresses, and label your father if he isn't rich, and insult you when your nose isn't nice."

"If you mean *libel,* I'd say so, and not talk about *labels,* as if Papa was a pickle bottle," advised Jo, laughing.

"I know what I mean, and you needn't be *statirical* about it. It's proper to use good words, and improve your *vocabilary,*" returned Amy, with dignity.

"Don't peck at one another, children. Don't you wish we had the money Papa lost when we were little, Jo? Dear me! how happy and good we'd be, if we had no worries!" said Meg, who could remember better times.

"You said the other day you thought we were a deal happier than the King children, for they were fighting and fretting all the time, in spite of their money."

"So I did, Beth. Well, I think we are; for, though we do have to work, we make fun for ourselves, and are a pretty jolly set, as Jo would say."

"Jo does use such slang words!" observed Amy, with a reproving look at the long figure stretched on the rug. Jo immediately sat up, put her hands in her pockets, and began to whistle.

"Don't, Jo, it's so boyish!"

"That's why I do it."

"I detest rude, unladylike girls!"

"I hate affected, niminy-piminy chits!"

" 'Birds in their little nests agree,' " sang Beth, the peacemaker, with such a funny face that both sharp voices softened to a laugh, and the "pecking" ended for that time.

"Really, girls, you are both to blame," said Meg, beginning to lecture in her elder-sisterly fashion. "You are old enough to leave off boyish tricks, and to behave better, Josephine. It didn't matter so much when you were a little girl; but now you are so tall, and turn up your hair, you should remember that you are a young lady."

"I'm not! And if turning up my hair makes me one, I'll wear it in two tails till I'm twenty," cried Jo, pulling off her net, and shaking down a chestnut mane. "I hate to think I've got to grow up, and be Miss March, and wear long gowns, and look as prim as a China aster! It's bad enough to be a girl, anyway, when I like boys' games and work and manners! I can't get over my disappointment in not being a boy; and it's worse than ever now, for I'm dying to go and fight with Papa, and I can only stay at home and knit, like a poky old woman!" And Jo shook the blue army sock till the needles rattled like castanets, and her ball bounded across the room.

"Poor Jo! It's too bad, but it can't be helped. So you must try to be contented with making your name boyish, and playing brother to us girls," said Beth, stroking the rough head at her knee with a hand that all the dishwashing and dusting in the world could not make ungentle in its touch.

"As for you, Amy," continued Meg, "you are altogether too particular and prim. Your airs are funny now, but you'll grow up an affected little goose, if you don't take care. I like your nice manners and refined ways of speaking, when you don't try to be elegant. But your absurd words are as bad as Jo's slang."

"If Jo is a tomboy and Amy a goose, what am I, please?" asked Beth, ready to share the lecture.

"You're a dear, and nothing else," answered Meg warmly; and no one contradicted her, for the "Mouse" was the pet of the family.

As young readers like to know "how people look," we will take this moment to give them a little sketch of the four sisters, who sat knitting away in the twilight, while the December snow fell quietly without, and the fire crackled cheerfully within. It was a comfortable old room, though the carpet was faded and the furniture very plain; for a good picture or two hung on the walls, books filled the recesses, chrysanthemums and Christmas roses bloomed in the windows, and a pleasant atmosphere of home peace pervaded it.

Margaret, the eldest of the four, was sixteen, and very pretty, being plump and fair, with large eyes, plenty of soft, brown hair, a sweet mouth, and white hands, of which she was rather vain. Fifteen-year-old Jo was very tall, thin, and brown, and reminded one of a colt, for she never seemed to know what to do with her long limbs, which were very much in her way. She had a decided mouth, a comical nose, and sharp, gray eyes, which appeared to see everything, and were by turns fierce, funny, or thoughtful. Her long, thick hair was her one beauty, but it was usually bundled into a net, to be out of her way. Round shoulders had Jo, big hands and feet, a flyaway look to her clothes, and the uncomfortable appearance of a girl who was rapidly shooting up into a woman and didn't like it. Elizabeth—or Beth, as everyone called her—was a rosy, smooth-haired, bright-eyed girl of thirteen, with a shy manner, a timid voice, and a peaceful expression which was seldom disturbed. Her father called her "Little Tranquillity," and the name suited her excellently, for she seemed to live in a happy world of her own, only venturing out to meet the few whom she trusted and loved. Amy, though the youngest, was a most important person—in her own opinion at least. A regular snow maiden, with blue eyes, and yellow hair curling on her shoulders, pale and slender, and always carrying herself like a young lady mindful of her manners. What the characters of the four sisters were we will leave to be found out.

The clock struck six and, having swept up the hearth, Beth put a pair of slippers down to warm. Somehow the sight of the old shoes had a good effect upon the girls, for Mother was coming, and everyone brightened to welcome her. Meg stopped lecturing, and lighted the lamp, Amy got out of the easy chair without being asked, and Jo forgot how tired she was as she sat up to hold the slippers nearer to the blaze.

"They are quite worn out. Marmee must have a new pair."

"I thought I'd get her some with my dollar," said Beth.

"No, I shall!" cried Amy.

"I'm the oldest," began Meg, but Jo cut in with a decided—

"I'm the man of the family now Papa is away, and *I* shall provide the slippers, for he told me to take special care of Mother while he was gone."

"I'll tell you what we'll do," said Beth, "let's each get her something for Christmas, and not get anything for ourselves."

"That's like you, dear! What will we get?" exclaimed Jo.

Everyone thought soberly for a minute, then Meg announced, as if the idea was suggested by the sight of her own pretty hands, "I shall give her a nice pair of gloves."

"Army shoes, best to be had," cried Jo.

"Some handkerchiefs, all hemmed," said Beth.

"I'll get a little bottle of cologne. She likes it, and it won't cost much, so I'll have some left to buy my pencils," added Amy.

"How will we give the things?" asked Meg.

"Put them on the table, and bring her in and see her open the bundles. Don't you remember how we used to do on our birthdays?" answered Jo.

"I used to be *so* frightened when it was my turn to sit in the big chair with the crown on, and see you all come marching round to give the presents, with a kiss. I liked the things and the kisses, but it was dreadful to have you sit looking at me while I opened the bundles," said Beth, who was toasting her face and the bread for tea at the same time.

"Let Marmee think we are getting things for ourselves, and then surprise her. We must go shopping tomorrow afternoon, Meg. There is so much to do about the play for Christmas night," said Jo, marching up and down, with her hands behind her back and her nose in the air.

"I don't mean to act any more after this time. I'm getting too old for such things," observed Meg, who was as much a child as ever about "dressing-up" frolics.

"You won't stop, I know, as long as you can trail round in a white gown with your hair down, and wear gold-paper jewelry. You are the best actress we've got, and there'll be an end of everything if you quit the boards," said Jo. "We ought to rehearse tonight. Come here, Amy, and do the fainting scene, for you are as stiff as a poker in that."

"I can't help it; I never saw anyone faint, and I don't choose to make myself all black and blue, tumbling flat as you do. If I can go down easily, I'll drop; if I can't, I shall fall into a chair and be graceful. I don't care if Hugo does come at me with a pistol," returned Amy, who was not gifted with dramatic power, but was chosen because she was small enough to be borne out shrieking by the villain of the piece.

"Do it this way: clasp your hands so, and stagger across the room, crying frantically, 'Roderigo! save me! save me!' " and away went Jo, with a melodramatic scream which was truly thrilling.

Amy followed, but she poked her hands out stiffly before her, and jerked herself along as if she went by machinery, and her "Ow!" was more suggestive of pins being run into her than of fear and anguish. Jo gave a despairing groan, and Meg laughed outright, while Beth let her bread burn as she watched the fun with interest.

"It's no use! Do the best you can when the time comes, and if the audience laughs, don't blame me. Come on, Meg."

Then things went smoothly, for Don Pedro defied the world in a speech of two pages without a single break; Hagar, the witch, chanted an awful incantation over her kettleful of simmering toads, with weird effect; Roderigo rent his chains asunder manfully, and Hugo died in agonies of remorse and arsenic, with a wild "Ha! ha!"

"It's the best we've had yet," said Meg, as the dead villain sat up and rubbed his elbows.

"I don't see how you can write and act such splendid things, Jo. You're a regular Shakespeare!" exclaimed Beth, who firmly believed that her sisters were gifted with wonderful genius in all things.

"Not quite," replied Jo modestly. "I do think *The Witch's Curse, an Operatic Tragedy* is rather a nice thing, but I'd like to try *Macbeth,* if we only had a trapdoor for Banquo. I always wanted to do the killing part. 'Is that a dagger that I see before me?' " muttered Jo, rolling her eyes and clutching at the air, as she had seen a famous tragedian do.

"No, it's the toasting fork, with mother's shoe on it instead of the bread. Beth's stage-struck!" cried Meg, and the rehearsal ended in a general burst of laughter.

"Glad to find you so merry, my girls," said a cheery voice at the door, and actors and audience turned to welcome a tall, motherly lady with a "can-I-help-you" look about her which was truly delightful. She was not elegantly dressed, but a noble-looking woman, and the girls thought the gray cloak and unfashionable bonnet covered the most splendid mother in the world.

"Well, dearies, how have you got on today? There was so much to do, getting the boxes ready to go tomorrow, that I didn't come home to dinner. Has anyone called, Beth? How is your cold, Meg? Jo, you look tired to death. Come and kiss me, baby."

While making these maternal inquiries Mrs. March got her wet things off, her warm slippers on, and sitting down in the easy chair, drew Amy to her lap, preparing to enjoy the happiest hour of her busy day. The girls flew about, trying to make things comfortable, each in her own way. Meg arranged the tea table, Jo brought wood and set chairs, dropping, overturning, and clattering everything she touched, Beth trotted to and fro between parlor and kitchen, quiet and busy, while Amy gave directions to everyone, as she sat with her hands folded.

As they gathered about the table, Mrs. March said, with a particularly happy face, "I've got a treat for you after supper."

A quick, bright smile went round like a streak of sunshine. Beth clapped her hands, regardless of the biscuit she held, and Jo tossed up her napkin, crying, "A letter! a letter! Three cheers for Father!"

"Yes, a nice long letter. He is well, and thinks he shall get through the cold season better than we feared. He sends all sorts of loving wishes for Christmas, and an especial message to you girls," said Mrs. March, patting her pocket as if she had got a treasure there.

"Hurry and get done! Don't stop to quirk your little finger and simper over your plate, Amy," cried Jo, choking in her tea and dropping her bread, butter side down, on the carpet in her haste to get at the treat.

Beth ate no more, but crept away to sit in her shadowy corner and brood over the delight to come, till the others were ready.

"I think it was so splendid in Father to go as a chaplain when he was too old to be drafted, and not strong enough for a soldier," said Meg warmly.

"Don't I wish I could go as a drummer, a *vivan*—what's its name? or a nurse, so I could be near him and help him," exclaimed Jo, with a groan.

"It must be very disagreeable to sleep in a tent, and eat all sorts of bad-tasting things, and drink out of a tin mug," sighed Amy.

"When will he come home, Marmee?" asked Beth, with a little quiver in her voice.

"Not for many months, dear, unless he is sick. He will stay and do his work faithfully as long as he can, and we won't ask for him back a minute sooner than he can be spared. Now come and hear the letter."

They all drew to the fire, Mother in the big chair with Beth at her feet, Meg and Amy perched on either arm of the chair, and Jo leaning on the back, where no one would see any sign of emotion if the letter should happen to be touching. Very few letters were written in those hard times that were not touching, especially those which fathers sent home. In this one little was said of the hardships endured, the dangers faced, or the homesickness conquered. It was a cheerful, hopeful letter, full of lively descriptions of camp life, marches, and military news, and only at the end did the writer's heart overflow with fatherly love and longing for the little girls at home.

"Give them all my dear love and a kiss. Tell them I think of them by day, pray for them by night, and find my best comfort in their affection at all times. A year seems very long to wait before I see them, but remind them that while we wait we may all work, so that these hard days need not be wasted. I know they will remember all

I said to them, that they will be loving children to you, will do their duty faithfully, fight their bosom enemies bravely, and conquer themselves so beautifully that when I come back to them I may be fonder and prouder than ever of my little women."

Everybody sniffed when they came to that part; Jo wasn't ashamed of the great tear that dropped off the end of her nose, and Amy never minded the rumpling of her curls as she hid her face on her mother's shoulder and sobbed out, "I *am* a selfish girl! but I'll truly try to be better, so he mayn't be disappointed in me by-and-by."

"We all will!" cried Meg. "I think too much of my looks and hate to work, but won't any more, if I can help it."

"I'll try and be what he loves to call me, 'a little woman,' and not be rough and wild, but do my duty here instead of wanting to be somewhere else," said Jo, thinking that keeping her temper at home was a much harder task than facing a rebel or two down South.

Beth said nothing, but wiped away her tears with the blue army sock and began to knit with all her might, losing no time in doing the duty that lay nearest her, while she resolved in her quiet little soul to be all that Father hoped to find her when the year brought round the happy coming home.

Mrs. March broke the silence that followed Jo's words, by saying in her cheery voice, "Do you remember how you used to play Pilgrim's Progress when you were little things? Nothing delighted you more than to have me tie my piece bags on your backs for burdens, give you hats and sticks and rolls of paper, and let you travel through the house from the cellar, which was the City of Destruction, up, up, to the housetop, where you had all the lovely things you could collect to make a Celestial City."

"What fun it was, especially going by the lions, fighting Apollyon, and passing through the Valley where the hobgoblins were!" said Jo.

"I liked the place where the bundles fell off and tumbled downstairs," said Meg.

"My favorite part was when we came out on the flat roof where our flowers and arbors and pretty things were, and all stood and sung for joy up there in the sunshine," said Beth, smiling, as if that pleasant moment had come back to her.

"I don't remember much about it, except that I was afraid of the cellar and the dark entry, and always liked the cake and milk we had up at the top. If I wasn't too old for such things, I'd rather like to play it over again," said Amy, who began to talk of renouncing childish things at the mature age of twelve.

"We never are too old for this, my dear, because it is a play we are playing all the time in one way or another. Our burdens are here, our road is before us, and the longing for goodness and happiness is the guide that leads us through many troubles and mistakes to the peace which is a true Celestial City. Now, my little pilgrims, suppose you begin again, not in play, but in earnest, and see how far on you can get before Father comes home."

"Really, Mother? Where are our bundles?" asked Amy, who was a very literal young lady.

"Each of you told what your burden was just now, except Beth. I rather think she hasn't got any," said her mother.

"Yes, I have. Mine is dishes and dusters, and envying girls with nice pianos, and being afraid of people."

Beth's bundle was such a funny one that everybody wanted to laugh, but nobody did, for it would have hurt her feelings very much.

"Let us do it," said Meg thoughtfully. "It is only another name for trying to be good, and the story may help us; for though we do want to be good, it's hard work and we forget, and don't do our best."

"We were in the Slough of Despond tonight, and Mother came and pulled us out as Help did in the book. We ought to have our roll of directions, like Christian. What shall we do about that?" asked Jo, delighted with the fancy which lent a little romance to the very dull task of doing her duty.

"Look under your pillows Christmas morning, and you will find your guidebook," replied Mrs. March.

They talked over the new plan while old Hannah cleared the table, then out came the four little workbaskets, and the needles flew as the girls made sheets for Aunt March. It was uninteresting sewing, but tonight no one grumbled. They adopted Jo's plan of dividing the long seams into four parts, and calling the quarters Europe, Asia, Africa, and America, and in that way got on capitally, especially when they talked about the different countries as they stitched their way through them.

At nine they stopped work, and sang, as usual, before they went to bed. No one but Beth could get much music out of the old piano, but she had a way of softly touching the yellow keys and making a pleasant accompaniment to the simple songs they sang. Meg had a voice like a flute, and she and her mother led the little choir. Amy chirped like a cricket, and Jo wandered through the airs at her own sweet will, always coming out at the wrong place with a croak or a quaver that spoiled the most pensive tune. They had always done this from the time they could lisp

Crinkle, crinkle, 'ittle 'tar,

and it had become a household custom, for the mother was a born singer. The first sound in the morning was her voice as she went about the house singing like a lark, and the last sound at night was the same cheery sound, for the girls never grew too old for that familiar lullaby.

CHAPTER 2
A MERRY CHRISTMAS

Jo was the first to wake in the gray dawn of Christmas morning. No stockings hung at the fireplace, and for a moment she felt as much disappointed as she did long ago, when her little sock fell down because it was so crammed with goodies. Then she remembered her mother's promise and, slipping her hand under her pillow, drew out a little crimson-covered book. She knew it very well, for it was that beautiful old story of the best life ever lived, and Jo felt that it was a true guidebook for any pilgrim going the long journey. She woke Meg with a "Merry Christmas," and bade her see what was under her pillow. A green-covered book appeared, with the same picture inside, and a few words written by their mother, which made their one present very precious in their eyes. Presently Beth and Amy woke to rummage and find their little books also—one dove-colored, the other blue—and all sat looking at and talking about them, while the east grew rosy with the coming day.

In spite of her small vanities, Margaret had a sweet and pious nature, which unconsciously influenced her sisters, especially Jo, who loved her very tenderly, and obeyed her because her advice was so gently given.

"Girls," said Meg seriously, looking from the tumbled head beside her to the two little nightcapped ones in the room beyond, "Mother wants us to read and love and mind these books, and we must begin at once. We used to be faithful about it, but since Father went away and all this war trouble unsettled us, we have neglected many things. You can do as you please, but *I* shall keep my book on the table here and read a little every morning as soon as I wake, for I know it will do me good and help me through the day."

Then she opened her new book and began to read. Jo put her arm round her and, leaning cheek to cheek, read also, with the quiet expression so seldom seen on her restless face.

"How good Meg is! Come, Amy, let's do as they do. I'll help you with the hard words, and they'll explain things if we don't understand," whispered Beth, very much impressed by the pretty books and her sisters' example.

"I'm glad mine is blue," said Amy. And then the rooms were very still while the pages were softly turned, and the winter sunshine crept in to touch the bright heads and serious faces with a Christmas greeting.

"Where is Mother?" asked Meg, as she and Jo ran down to thank her for their gifts, half an hour later.

"Goodness only knows. Some poor creeter come a-beggin', and your ma went straight off to see what was needed. There never *was* such a woman for givin' away vittles and drink, clothes and firin'," replied Hannah, who had lived with the family since Meg was born, and was considered by them all more as a friend than a servant.

"She will be back soon, I think, so fry your cakes, and have everything ready," said Meg, looking over the presents which were collected in a basket and kept under the sofa, ready to be produced at the proper time. "Why, where is Amy's bottle of cologne?" she added, as the little flask did not appear.

"She took it out a minute ago, and went off with it to put a ribbon on it, or some such notion," replied Jo, dancing about the room to take the first stiffness off the new army slippers.

"How nice my handkerchiefs look, don't they? Hannah washed and ironed them for me, and I marked them all myself," said Beth, looking proudly at the somewhat uneven letters which had cost her such labor.

"Bless the child! She's gone and put 'Mother' on them instead of 'M. March.' How funny!" cried Jo, taking up one.

"Isn't it right? I thought it was better to do it so, because Meg's initials are M. M., and I don't want anyone to use these but Marmee," said Beth, looking troubled.

"It's all right, dear, and a very pretty idea—quite sensible, too, for no one can ever mistake now. It will please her very much, I know," said Meg, with a frown for Jo and a smile for Beth.

"There's Mother. Hide the basket, quick!" cried Jo, as a door slammed and steps sounded in the hall.

Amy came in hastily, and looked rather abashed when she saw her sisters all waiting for her.

"Where have you been, and what are you hiding behind you?" asked Meg, surprised to see, by her hood and cloak, that lazy Amy had been out so early.

"Don't laugh at me, Jo! I didn't mean anyone should know till the time came. I only meant to change the little bottle for a big one, and I gave *all* my money to get it, and I'm truly trying not to be selfish any more."

As she spoke, Amy showed the handsome flask which replaced the cheap one, and looked so earnest and humble in her little effort to forget herself that Meg hugged her on the spot, and Jo pronounced her "a trump," while Beth ran to the window, and picked her finest rose to ornament the stately bottle.

"You see I felt ashamed of my present, after reading and talking about being good this morning, so I ran round the corner and changed it the minute I was up: and I'm *so* glad, for mine is the handsomest now."

Another bang of the street door sent the basket under the sofa, and the girls to the table, eager for breakfast.

"Merry Christmas, Marmee! Many of them! Thank you for our books; we read some, and mean to every day," they cried, in chorus.

"Merry Christmas, little daughters! I'm glad you began at once, and hope you will keep on. But I want to say one word before we sit down. Not far away from here lies a poor woman with a little newborn baby. Six children are huddled into one bed to keep from freezing, for they have no fire. There is nothing to eat over there, and the oldest boy came to tell me they were suffering hunger and cold. My girls, will you give them your breakfast as a Christmas present?"

They were all unusually hungry, having waited nearly an hour, and for a minute no one spoke—only a minute, for Jo exclaimed impetuously, "I'm so glad you came before we began!"

"May I go and help carry the things to the poor little children?" asked Beth eagerly.

"*I* shall take the cream and the muffins," added Amy, heroically giving up the articles she most liked.

Meg was already covering the buckwheats, and piling the bread into one big plate.

"I thought you'd do it," said Mrs. March, smiling as if satisfied. "You shall all go and help me, and when we come back we will have bread and milk for breakfast, and make it up at dinnertime."

They were soon ready, and the procession set out. Fortunately it was early, and they went through back streets, so few people saw them, and no one laughed at the queer party.

A poor, bare, miserable room it was, with broken windows, no fire, ragged bedclothes, a sick mother, wailing baby, and a group of pale, hungry children cuddled under one old quilt, trying to keep warm.

How the big eyes stared and the blue lips smiled as the girls went in!

"*Ach, mein Gott!* It is good angels come to us!" said the poor woman, crying for joy.

"Funny angels in hoods and mittens," said Jo, and set them laughing.

In a few minutes it really did seem as if kind spirits had been at work there. Hannah, who had carried wood, made a fire, and stopped up the broken panes with old hats and her own cloak. Mrs. March gave the mother tea and gruel, and comforted her with promises of help, while she dressed the little baby as tenderly as if it had been her own. The girls meantime spread the table, set the children round the fire, and fed them like so many hungry birds—laughing, talking, and trying to understand the funny broken English.

"Das ist gut!" "Die Engel-kinder!" cried the poor things as they ate and warmed their purple hands at the comfortable blaze.

The girls had never been called angel children before, and thought it very agreeable, especially Jo, who had been considered a "Sancho" ever since she was born. That was a very happy breakfast, though they didn't get any of it; and when they went away, leaving comfort behind, I think there were not in all the city four merrier people than the hungry little girls who gave away their breakfasts and contented themselves with bread and milk on Christmas morning.

"That's loving our neighbor better than ourselves, and I like it," said Meg, as they set out their presents while their mother was upstairs collecting clothes for the poor Hummels.

Not a very splendid show, but there was a great deal of love done up in the few little bundles, and the tall vase of red roses, white chrysanthemums, and trailing vines, which stood in the middle, gave quite an elegant air to the table.

"She's coming! Strike up, Beth! Open the door, Amy! Three cheers for Marmee!" cried Jo, prancing about while Meg went to conduct Mother to the seat of honor.

Beth played her gayest march, Amy threw open the door, and Meg enacted escort with great dignity. Mrs. March was both surprised and touched, and smiled with her eyes full as she examined her presents and read the little notes which accompanied them. The slippers went on at once, a new handkerchief was slipped into her pocket, well scented with Amy's cologne, the rose was fastened in her bosom, and the nice gloves were pronounced a "perfect fit."

There was a good deal of laughing and kissing and explaining, in the simple, loving fashion which makes these home festivals so pleasant at the time, so sweet to remember long afterward, and then all fell to work.

The morning charities and ceremonies took so much time that the rest of the day was devoted to preparations for the evening festivities. Being still too young to go often to the theater, and not rich enough to afford any great outlay for private performances, the girls put their wits to work, and—necessity being the mother of invention—made whatever they needed. Very clever were some of their productions—pasteboard guitars, antique lamps made of old-fashioned butter boats covered with silver paper, gorgeous robes of old cotton, glittering with tin spangles from a pickle factory, and armor covered with the same useful diamond-shaped bits left in sheets when the lids of tin preserve pots were cut out. The furniture was used to being turned topsy-turvy, and the big chamber was the scene of many innocent revels.

No gentlemen were admitted, so Jo played male parts to her heart's content and took immense satisfaction in a pair of russet-leather boots given her by a friend, who knew a lady who knew an actor. These boots, an old foil, and a slashed doublet once used by an artist for some picture, were Jo's chief treasures and appeared on all occasions. The smallness of the company made it necessary for the two principal actors to take several parts apiece, and they certainly deserved some credit for the hard work they did in learning three or four different parts, whisking in and out of various costumes, and managing the stage besides. It was excellent drill for their memories, a harmless amusement, and employed many hours which otherwise would have been idle, lonely, or spent in less profitable society.

On Christmas night, a dozen girls piled onto the bed which was the dress circle, and sat before the blue and yellow chintz curtains in a most flattering state of expectancy. There was a good deal of rustling and whispering behind the curtain, a trifle of lamp smoke, and an occasional giggle from Amy, who was apt to get hysterical in the excitement of the moment. Presently a bell sounded, the curtains flew apart, and the *Operatic Tragedy* began.

"A gloomy wood," according to the one playbill, was represented by a few scrubs in pots, green baize on the floor, and a cave in the distance. This cave was made with a clotheshorse for a roof, bureaus for walls, and in it was a small furnace in full blast, with a black pot on it and an old witch bending over it. The stage was dark and the glow of the furnace had a fine effect, especially as real steam issued from the kettle when the witch took off the cover. A moment was allowed for the first thrill to subside, then Hugo, the villain, stalked in with a clanking sword at his side, a slouched hat, black beard, mysterious cloak, and the boots. After pacing to and fro in much agitation, he struck his forehead, and burst out in a wild strain, singing of his hatred of Roderigo, his love for Zara, and his pleasing resolution to kill the one and win the other. The gruff tones of Hugo's voice, with an occasional shout when his feelings overcame him, were very impressive, and the audience applauded the moment he paused for breath. Bowing with the air of one accustomed to public praise, he stole to the cavern and ordered Hagar to come forth with a commanding, "What ho, minion! I need thee!"

Out came Meg, with gray horsehair hanging about her face, a red and black robe, a staff, and cabalistic signs upon her cloak. Hugo demanded a potion to make Zara adore him, and one to destroy Roderigo. Hagar, in a fine dramatic melody, promised both, and proceeded to call up the spirit who would bring the love philter:

Hither, hither, from thy home,
Airy sprite, I bid thee come!
Born of roses, fed on dew,
Charms and potions canst thou brew?
Bring me here, with elfin speed,
The fragrant philter which I need;
Make it sweet and swift and strong,
Spirit, answer now my song!

A soft strain of music sounded, and then at the back of the cave appeared a little figure in cloudy white, with glittering wings, golden hair, and a garland of roses on its head. Waving a wand, it sang,

Hither I come,
From my airy home,
Afar in the silver moon.
Take the magic spell,
And use it well,
Or its power will vanish soon!

And dropping a small, gilded bottle at the witch's feet, the spirit vanished. Another chant from Hagar produced another apparition—not a lovely one, for with a bang an ugly black imp appeared and, having croaked a reply, tossed a dark bottle at Hugo and disappeared with a mocking laugh. Having warbled his thanks and put the potions in his boots, Hugo departed, and Hagar informed the audience that, as he had killed a few of her friends in times past, she has cursed him, and intends to thwart his plans, and be revenged on him. Then the curtain fell, and the audience reposed and ate candy while discussing the merits of the play.

A good deal of hammering went on before the curtain rose again, but when it became evident what a masterpiece of stage carpentering had been got up, no one murmured at the delay. It was truly superb! A tower rose to the ceiling; halfway up appeared a window with a lamp burning at it, and behind the white curtain appeared Zara in a lovely blue and silver dress, waiting for Roderigo. He came in gorgeous array, with plumed cap, red cloak, chestnut lovelocks, a guitar, and the boots, of course. Kneeling at the foot of the tower, he sang a serenade in melting tones. Zara replied and, after a musical dialogue, consented to fly. Then came the grand effect of the play. Roderigo produced a rope ladder, with five steps to it, threw up one end, and invited Zara to descend. Timidly she crept from her lattice, put her hand on Roderigo's shoulder, and was about to leap gracefully down when "Alas! alas for Zara!" she forgot her train—it caught in the window, the tower tottered, leaned forward, fell with a crash, and buried the unhappy lovers in the ruins!

A universal shriek arose as the russet boots waved wildly from the wreck and a golden head emerged, exclaiming, "I told you so! I told you so!" With wonderful presence of mind, Don Pedro, the cruel sire, rushed in, dragged out his daughter, with a hasty aside—

"Don't laugh! Act as if it was all right!"—and, ordering Roderigo up, banished him from the kingdom with wrath and scorn. Though decidedly shaken by the fall of the tower upon him, Roderigo defied the old gentleman and refused to stir. This dauntless example fired Zara: she also defied her sire, and he ordered them both to the deepest dungeons of the castle. A stout little retainer came in with chains and led them away, looking very much frightened and evidently forgetting the speech he ought to have made.

Act third was the castle hall, and here Hagar appeared, having come to free the lovers and finish Hugo. She hears him coming and hides, sees him put the potions into two cups of wine and bid the timid little servant, "Bear them to the captives in their cells, and tell them I shall come anon." The servant takes Hugo aside to tell him something, and Hagar changes the cups for two others which are harmless. Ferdinando, the "minion," carries them away, and Hagar puts back the cup which holds the poison meant for Roderigo. Hugo, getting thirsty after a long warble, drinks it, loses his wits, and after a good deal of clutching and stamping, falls flat and dies, while Hagar informs him what she has done in a song of exquisite power and melody.

This was a truly thrilling scene, though some persons might have thought that the sudden tumbling down of a quantity of long hair rather marred the effect of the villain's death. He was called before the curtain, and with great propriety appeared, leading Hagar, whose singing was considered more wonderful than all the rest of the performance put together.

Act fourth displayed the despairing Roderigo on the point of stabbing himself because he has been told that Zara has deserted him. Just as the dagger is at his heart, a lovely song is sung under his window, informing him that Zara is true but in danger, and he can save her if he will. A key is thrown in, which unlocks the door, and in a spasm of rapture he tears off his chains and rushes away to find and rescue his ladylove.

Act fifth opened with a stormy scene between Zara and Don Pedro. He wishes her to go into a convent, but she won't hear of it and, after a touching appeal, is about to faint when Roderigo dashes in and demands her hand. Don Pedro refuses, because he is not rich. They shout and gesticulate tremendously but cannot agree, and Roderigo is about to bear away the exhausted Zara, when the timid servant enters with a letter and a bag from Hagar, who has mysteriously disappeared. The letter informs the party that she bequeaths untold wealth to the young pair and an awful doom to Don Pedro, if he doesn't make them happy. The bag is opened, and several quarts of tin money shower down upon the stage till it is quite glorified with the glitter. This entirely softens the "stern sire." He consents without a murmur, all join in a joyful chorus, and the curtain falls upon the lovers kneeling to receive Don Pedro's blessing in attitudes of the most romantic grace.

Tumultuous applause followed but received an unexpected check, for the cot bed, on which the "dress circle" was built, suddenly shut up and extinguished the enthusiastic audience. Roderigo and Don Pedro flew to the rescue, and all were taken out unhurt, though many were speechless with laughter. The excitement had hardly subsided when Hannah appeared, with "Mrs. March's compliments, and would the ladies walk down to supper."

This was a surprise even to the actors, and when they saw the table, they looked at one another in rapturous amazement. It was like Marmee to get up a little treat for them, but anything so fine as this was unheard of since the departed days of plenty. There was ice cream—actually two dishes of it, pink and white—and cake and fruit and distracting French bonbons and, in the middle of the table, four great bouquets of hothouse flowers!

It quite took their breath away; and they stared first at the table and then at their mother, who looked as if she enjoyed it immensely.

"Is it fairies?" asked Amy.

"It's Santa Claus," said Beth.

"Mother did it." And Meg smiled her sweetest, in spite of her gray beard and white eyebrows.

"Aunt March had a good fit and sent the supper," cried Jo, with a sudden inspiration.

"All wrong. Old Mr. Laurence sent it," replied Mrs. March.

"The Laurence boy's grandfather! What in the world put such a thing into his head? We don't know him!" exclaimed Meg.

"Hannah told one of his servants about your breakfast party. He is an odd old gentleman, but that pleased him. He knew my father years ago, and he sent me a polite note this afternoon, saying he hoped I would allow him to express his friendly feeling toward my children by sending them a few trifles in honor of the day. I could not refuse, and so you have a little feast at night to make up for the bread-and-milk breakfast."

"That boy put it into his head, I know he did! He's a capital fellow, and I wish we could get acquainted. He looks as if he'd like to know us but he's bashful, and Meg is so prim she won't let me speak to him when we pass," said Jo, as the plates went round, and the ice began to melt out of sight, with ohs and ahs of satisfaction.

"You mean the people who live in the big house next door, don't you?" asked one of the girls. "My mother knows old Mr. Laurence, but says he's very proud and doesn't like to mix with his neighbors. He keeps his grandson shut up, when he isn't riding or walking with his tutor, and makes him study very hard. We invited him to our party, but he didn't come. Mother says he's very nice, though he never speaks to us girls."

"Our cat ran away once, and he brought her back, and we talked over the fence, and were getting on capitally—all about cricket, and so on—when he saw Meg coming, and walked off. I mean to know him some day, for he needs fun, I'm sure he does," said Jo decidedly.

"I like his manners, and he looks like a little gentleman; so I've no objection to your knowing him, if a proper opportunity comes. He brought the flowers himself, and I should have asked him in, if I had been sure what was going on upstairs. He looked so wistful as he went away, hearing the frolic and evidently having none of his own."

"It's a mercy you didn't, Mother!" laughed Jo, looking at her boots. "But we'll have another play sometime that he *can* see. Perhaps he'll help act. Wouldn't that be jolly?"

"I never had such a fine bouquet before! How pretty it is!" And Meg examined her flowers with great interest.

"They *are* lovely! But Beth's roses are sweeter to me," said Mrs. March, smelling the half-dead posy in her belt.

Beth nestled up to her, and whispered softly, "I wish I could send my bunch to Father. I'm afraid he isn't having such a merry Christmas as we are."

From
The Pickwick Papers

CHAPTER 28

A good-humoured Christmas Chapter, containing an Account of a Wedding, and some other Sports beside: which although in their way, even as good Customs as Marriage itself, are not quite so religiously kept up, in these degenerate Times

As brisk as bees, if not altogether as light as fairies, did the four Pickwickians assemble on the morning of the twenty-second day of December, in the year of grace in which these, their faithfully-recorded adventures, were undertaken and accomplished. Christmas was close at hand, in all his bluff and hearty honesty; it was the season of hospitality, merriment, and open-heartedness; the old year was preparing, like an ancient philosopher, to call his friends around him, and amidst the sound of feasting and revelry to pass gently and calmly away. Gay and merry was the time, and gay and merry were at least four of the numerous hearts that were gladdened by its coming.

And numerous indeed are the hearts to which Christmas brings a brief season of happiness and enjoyment. How many families, whose members have been dispersed and scattered far and wide, in the restless struggles of life, are then re-united, and meet once again in that happy state of companionship and mutual good-will, which is a source of such pure and unalloyed delight, and one so incompatible with the cares and sorrows of the world, that the religious belief of the most civilised nations, and the rude traditions of the roughest savages, alike number it among the first joys of a future condition of existence, provided for the blest and happy! How many old recollections, and how many dormant sympathies, does Christmas time awaken!

We write these words now, many miles distant from the spot at which, year after year, we met on that day, a merry and joyous circle. Many of the hearts that throbbed so gaily then, have ceased to beat; many of the looks that shone so brightly then, have ceased to glow; the hands we grasped have grown cold; the eyes we sought have hid their lustre in the grave; and yet the old house, the room, the merry voices and smiling faces, the jest, the laugh, the most minute and trivial circumstances connected with those happy meetings, crowd upon our mind at each recurrence of the season, as if the last assemblage had been but yesterday! Happy, happy Christmas, that can win us back to the delusions of our childish days; that can recall to the old man the pleasures of his youth; that can transport the sailor and the traveller, thousands of miles away, back to his own fire-side and his quiet home!

But we are so taken up and occupied with the good qualities of this saint Christmas, that we are keeping Mr. Pickwick and his friends waiting in the cold on the outside of the Muggleton coach, which they have just attained, well wrapped up in great-coats, shawls, and comforters. The portmanteaus and carpet-bags have been stowed away, and Mr. Weller and the guard are endeavouring to insinuate into the fore-boot a huge cod-fish several sizes too large for it—which is snugly packed up, in a long brown basket, with a layer of straw over the top, and which has been left to the last, in order that he may repose in safety on the half-dozen barrels of real native oysters, all the property of Mr. Pickwick, which have been arranged in regular order at the bottom of the receptacle. The interest displayed in Mr. Pickwick's countenance is most intense, as Mr. Weller and the guard try to squeeze the cod-fish into the boot, first head first, and then tail first, and then top upward, and then bottom upward, and then side-ways, and then long-ways, all of which artifices the implacable cod-fish sturdily resists, until the guard accidentally hits him in the very middle of the basket, whereupon he suddenly disappears into the boot, and with him, the head and shoulders of the guard himself, who, not calculating upon so sudden a cessation of the passive resistance of the cod-fish, experiences a very unexpected shock, to the unsmotherable delight of all the porters and bystanders. Upon this, Mr. Pickwick smiles with great good-humour, and drawing a shilling from his waistcoat pocket, begs the guard, as he picks himself out of the boot, to drink his health in a glass of hot brandy and water; at which the guard smiles too, and Messrs. Snodgrass, Winkle, and Tupman, all smile in company. The guard and Mr. Weller disappear for five minutes: most probably to get the hot brandy and water, for they smell very strongly of it, when they return, the coachman mounts to the box, Mr. Weller jumps up behind, the Pickwickians pull their coats round their legs and their shawls over their noses, the helpers pull the horse-cloths off, the coachman shouts out a cheery "All right," and away they go.

They have rumbled through the streets, and jolted over the stones, and at length reach the wide and open country. The wheels skim over the hard and frosty ground: and the horses, bursting into a canter at a smart crack of the whip, step along the road as if the load behind them: coach, passengers, cod-fish, oyster barrels, and all: were but a feather at their heels. They have descended a gentle slope, and enter upon a level, as compact and dry as a solid block of marble, two miles long. Another crack of the whip, and on they speed, at a smart gallop: the horses tossing their heads and rattling the harness, as if in exhilaration at the rapidity of the motion: while the coachman, holding whip and reins in one hand, takes off his hat with the other, and resting it on his knees, pulls out his handkerchief, and wipes his forehead: partly because he has a habit of doing it, and partly because it's as well to show the passengers how cool he is, and what an easy thing it is to drive four-in-hand, when you have had as much practice as he has. Having done this very leisurely (otherwise the effect would be materially impaired), he replaces his handkerchief, pulls on his hat, adjusts his gloves, squares his elbows, cracks the whip again, and on they speed, more merrily than before.

STORIES

O. Henry was the pen name of William Sydney Porter (1862–1910). "The Gift of the Magi," among the best known of his numerous short stories, was first published in the collection The Four Million *(a reference to the population of New York City at the time) in 1906.*

The Danish storyteller Hans Christian Andersen was born in 1805 and produced a famous set of fairy stories with significant moral overtones and mythical importance. He died in 1875.

The sleuth Sherlock Holmes and his sidekick, Dr. Watson, were the creations of Sir Arthur Conan Doyle (1859–1930). At Christmastime in London, the Countess of Morcar's blue carbuncle, a fabulous precious stone, has been stolen and a Christmas goose left in Tottenham Court Road. Holmes and Watson will investigate.

The Gift of the Magi

O. Henry

One dollar and eighty-seven cents. That was all. And sixty cents of it was in pennies. Pennies saved one and two at a time by bulldozing the grocer and the vegetable man and the butcher until one's cheeks burned with the silent imputation of parsimony that such close dealing implied. Three times Della counted it. One dollar and eighty-seven cents. And the next day would be Christmas.

There was clearly nothing to do but flop down on the shabby little couch and howl. So Della did it. Which instigates the moral reflection that life is made up of sobs, sniffles, and smiles, with sniffles predominating.

While the mistress of the home is gradually subsiding from the first stage to the second, take a look at the home. A furnished flat at $8 per week. It did not exactly beggar description, but it certainly had that word on the lookout for the mendicancy squad.

In the vestibule below was a letter-box into which no letter would go, and an electric button from which no mortal finger could coax a ring. Also appertaining thereunto was a card bearing the name "Mr. James Dillingham Young."

The "Dillingham" had been flung to the breeze during a former period of prosperity when its possessor was being paid $30 per week. Now, when the income was shrunk to $20, the letters of "Dillingham" looked blurred, as though they were thinking seriously of contracting to a modest and unassuming D. But whenever Mr. James Dillingham Young came home and reached his flat above he was called "Jim" and greatly hugged by Mrs. James Dillingham Young, already introduced to you as Della. Which is all very good.

Della finished her cry and attended to her cheeks with the powder rag. She stood by the window and looked out dully at a gray cat walking a gray fence in a gray backyard. Tomorrow would be Christmas Day and she had only $1.87 with which to buy Jim a present. She had been saving every penny she could for months, with this result. Twenty dollars a week doesn't go far. Expenses had been greater than she had calculated. They always are. Only $1.87 to buy a present for Jim. Her Jim. Many a happy hour she had spent planning for something nice for him. Something fine and rare and sterling—something just a little bit near to being worthy of the honor of being owned by Jim.

There was a pier-glass between the windows of the room. Perhaps you have seen a pier-glass in an $8 flat. A very thin and very agile person may, by observing his reflection in a rapid sequence of longitudinal strips, obtain a fairly accurate conception of his looks. Della, being slender, had mastered the art.

Suddenly she whirled from the window and stood before the glass. Her eyes were shining brilliantly, but her face had lost its color within twenty seconds. Rapidly she pulled down her hair and let it fall to its full length.

Now, there were two possessions of the James Dillingham Youngs in which they both took a mighty pride. One was Jim's gold watch that had been his father's and his grandfather's. The other was Della's hair. Had the Queen of Sheba lived in the flat across the airshaft, Della would have let her hair hang out the window some day to dry just to depreciate Her Majesty's jewels and gifts. Had King Solomon been the janitor, with all his treasures piled up in the basement, Jim would have pulled out his watch every time he passed, just to see him pluck at his beard from envy.

So now Della's beautiful hair fell about her rippling and shining like a cascade of brown waters. It reached below her knee and made itself almost a garment for her. And then she did it up again nervously and quickly. Once she faltered for a minute and stood still while a tear or two splashed on the worn red carpet.

On went her old brown jacket; on went her old brown hat. With a whirl of skirts and with the brilliant sparkle still in her eyes, she fluttered out the door and down the stairs to the street.

Where she stopped the sign read: "Mme. Sofronie. Hair Goods of All Kinds." One flight up Della ran, and collected herself, panting. Madame, large, too white, chilly, hardly looked the "Sofronie."

"Will you buy my hair?" asked Della.

"I buy hair," said Madame. "Take yer hat off and let's have a sight at the looks of it."

Down rippled the brown cascade.

"Twenty dollars," said Madame, lifting the mass with a practised hand.

"Give it to me quick," said Della.

Oh, and the next two hours tripped by on rosy wings. Forget the hashed metaphor. She was ransacking the stores for Jim's present.

She found it at last. It surely had been made for Jim and no one else. There was no other like it in any of the stores, and she had turned all of them inside out. It was a platinum fob chain simple and chaste in design, properly proclaiming its value by substance alone and not by meretricious ornamentation—as all good things should do. It was even worthy of The Watch. As soon as she saw it she knew that it must be Jim's. It was like him. Quietness and value—the description applied to both. Twenty-one dollars they took from her for it, and she hurried home with the 87 cents. With that chain on his watch Jim might be properly anxious about the time in any company. Grand as the watch was, he sometimes looked at it on the sly on account of the old leather strap that he used in place of a chain.

When Della reached home her intoxication gave way a little to prudence and reason. She got out her curling irons and lighted the gas and went to work repairing the ravages made by generosity added to love. Which is always a tremendous task, dear friends—a mammoth task.

Within forty minutes her head was covered with tiny, close-lying curls that made her look wonderfully like a truant schoolboy. She looked at her reflection in the mirror long, carefully, and critically.

"If Jim doesn't kill me," she said to herself, "before he takes a second look at me, he'll say I look like a Coney Island chorus girl. But what could I do—oh! what could I do with a dollar and eighty-seven cents?"

At 7 o'clock the coffee was made and the frying-pan was on the back of the stove hot and ready to cook the chops.

Jim was never late. Della doubled the fob chain in her hand and sat on the corner of the table near the door that he always entered. Then she heard his step on the stair away down on the first flight, and she turned white for just a moment. She had a habit of saying little silent prayers about the simplest everyday things, and now she whispered: "Please God, make him think I am still pretty."

The door opened and Jim stepped in and closed it. He looked thin and very serious. Poor fellow, he was only twenty-two—and to be burdened with a family! He needed a new overcoat and he was without gloves.

Jim stepped inside the door, as immovable as a setter at the scent of quail. His eyes were fixed upon Della, and there was an expression in them that she could not read, and it terrified her. It was not anger, nor surprise, nor disapproval, nor horror, nor any of the sentiments that she had been prepared for. He simply stared at her fixedly with that peculiar expression on his face.

Della wriggled off the table and went for him.

"Jim, darling," she cried, "don't look at me that way. I had my hair cut off and sold it because I couldn't have lived through Christmas without giving you a present. It'll grow out again—you won't mind, will you? I just had to do it. My hair grows awfully fast. Say 'Merry Christmas!' Jim, and let's be happy. You don't know what a nice—what a beautiful, nice gift I've got for you."

"You've cut off your hair?" asked Jim, laboriously, as if he had not arrived at that patent fact yet even after the hardest mental labor.

"Cut it off and sold it," said Della. "Don't you like me just as well, anyhow? I'm me without my hair, ain't I?"

Jim looked about the room curiously.

"You say your hair is gone?" he said, with an air almost of idiocy.

"You needn't look for it," said Della. "It's sold, I tell you—sold and gone, too. It's Christmas Eve, boy. Be good to me, for it went for you. Maybe the hairs on my head were numbered," she went on with a sudden serious sweetness, "but nobody could ever count my love for you. Shall I put the chops on, Jim?"

Out of his trance Jim seemed quickly to wake. He enfolded his Della. For ten seconds let us regard with discreet scrutiny some inconsequential object in the other direction. Eight dollars a week or a million a year—what is the difference? A mathematician or a wit would give you the wrong answer. The Magi brought valuable gifts, but that was not among them. This dark assertion will be illuminated later on.

Jim drew a package from his overcoat pocket and threw it upon the table.

"Don't make any mistake, Dell," he said, "about me. I don't think there's anything in the way of a haircut or a shave or a shampoo that could make me like my girl any less. But if you'll unwrap that package you may see why you had me going a while at first."

White fingers and nimble tore at the string and paper. And then an ecstatic scream of joy; and then, alas! a quick feminine change to hysterical tears and wails, necessitating the immediate employment of all the comforting powers of the lord of the flat.

For there lay The Combs—the set of combs, side and back, that Della had worshipped for long in a Broadway window. Beautiful combs, pure tortoise shell, with jewelled rims—just the shade to wear in the beautiful vanished hair. They were expensive combs, she knew, and her heart had simply craved and yearned over them without the least hope of possession. And now, they were hers, but the tresses that should have adorned the coveted adornments were gone.

But she hugged them to her bosom, and at length she was able to look up with dim eyes and a smile and say: "My hair grows so fast, Jim!"

And then Della leaped up like a little singed cat and cried, "Oh, oh!"

Jim had not yet seen his beautiful present. She held it out to him eagerly upon her open palm. The dull precious metal seemed to flash with a reflection of her bright and ardent spirit.

"Isn't it a dandy, Jim? I hunted all over town to find it. You'll have to look at the time a hundred times a day now. Give me your watch. I want to see how it looks on it."

Instead of obeying, Jim tumbled down on the couch and put his hands under the back of his head and smiled.

"Dell," said he, "let's put our Christmas presents away and keep 'em a while. They're too nice to use just at present. I sold the watch to get the money to buy your combs. And now suppose you put the chops on."

The magi, as you know, were wise men—wonderfully wise men—who brought gifts to the Babe in the manger. They invented the art of giving Christmas presents. Being wise, their gifts were no doubt wise ones, possibly bearing the privilege of exchange in case of duplication. And here I have lamely related to you the uneventful chronicle of two foolish children in a flat who most unwisely sacrificed for each other the greatest treasures of their house. But in a last word to the wise of these days let it be said that of all who give gifts these two were the wisest. Of all who give and receive gifts, such as they are wisest. Everywhere they are wisest. They are the magi.

The Fir Tree

Hans Christian Andersen

Out in the woods stood a nice little Fir Tree. The place he had was a very good one; the sun shone on him; as to fresh air, there was enough of that, and round him grew many large-sized comrades, pines as well as firs. But the little Fir wanted so very much to be a grown-up tree.

He did not think of the warm sun and of the fresh air; he did not care for the little peasant children that ran about and prattled when they were in the woods looking for wild strawberries. The children often came with a whole pitcher full of berries, or a long row of them threaded on a straw, and sat down near the young Tree and said, "O, how pretty he is! what a nice little fir!" But this was what the Tree could not bear to hear.

At the end of a year he had shot up a good deal, and after another year he was another long bit taller; for with fir trees one can always tell by the shoots how many years old they are.

"O, were I but such a high tree as the others are," sighed he.

"Then I should be able to spread out my branches, and with the tops to look into the wide world! Then would the birds build nests among my branches; and when there was a breeze, I could bend with as much stateliness as the others!"

Neither the sunbeams, nor the birds, nor the red clouds which morning and evening sailed above him, gave the little Tree any pleasure.

In winter, when the snow lay glittering on the ground, a hare would often come leaping along, and jump right over the little Tree. O, that made him so angry! But two winters were past, and in the third the Tree was so large that the hare was obliged to go round it. "To grow and grow, to get older and be tall," thought the Tree, "that, after all, is the most delightful thing in the world!"

In autumn the wood-cutters always came and felled some of the largest trees. This happened every year; and the young Fir Tree, that had now grown to a very comely size, trembled at the sight; for the magnificent great trees fell to the earth with noise and cracking, the branches were lopped off, and the trees looked long and bare: they were hardly to be recognized; and then they were laid in carts, and the horses dragged them out of the wood.

Where did they go to? What became of them?

In spring, when the swallows and the storks came, the Tree asked them, "Don't you know where they have been taken? Have you not met them anywhere?"

The swallows did not know anything about it; but the Stork looked musing, nodded his head, and said, "Yes; I think I know; I met many ships as I was flying hither from Egypt; on the ships were magnificent masts, and I venture to assert that it was they that smelt so of fir. I may congratulate you, for they lifted themselves on high most majestically!"

"O, were I but old enough to fly across the sea! But how does the sea look in reality? What is it like?"

"That would take a long time to explain," said the Stork, and with these words off he went.

"Rejoice in thy growth!" said the sunbeams, "rejoice in thy vigorous growth, and in the fresh life that moveth within thee!"

And the wind kissed the Tree, and the dew wept tears over him; but the Fir understood it not.

When Christmas came, quite young trees were cut down; trees which often were not even as large or of the same age as this Fir Tree, who could never rest, but always wanted to be off. These young trees, and they were always the finest looking, retained their branches; they were laid on carts, and the horses drew them out of the wood.

"Where are they going to?" asked the Fir. "They are not taller than I; there was one indeed that was considerably shorter; and why do they retain all their branches? Whither are they taken?"

"We know! we know!" chirped the sparrows. "We have peeped in at the windows in the town below! We know whither they are taken! The greatest splendor and the greatest magnificence one can imagine await them. We peeped through the windows, and saw them planted in the middle of the warm room, and ornamented with the most splendid things—with gilded apples, with gingerbread, with toys, and many hundred lights!"

"And then?" asked the Fir Tree, trembling in every bough. "And then? What happens then?"

"We did not see anything more: it was incomparably beautiful."

"I would fain know if I am destined for so glorious a career," cried the Tree, rejoicing. "That is still better than to cross the sea! What a longing do I suffer! Were Christmas but come! I am now tall, and my branches spread like the others that were carried off last year! O, were I but already on the cart! Were I in the warm room with all the splendor and magnificence! Yes; then something better, something still grander, will surely follow, or wherefore should they thus ornament me? Something better, something still grander, *must* follow—but what? O, how I long, how I suffer! I do not know myself what is the matter with me!"

"Rejoice in our presence!" said the air and the sunlight; "rejoice in thy own fresh youth!"

But the Tree did not rejoice at all; he grew and grew, and was green both winter and summer. People that saw him said, "What a fine tree!" and towards Christmas he was one of the first that was cut down. The axe struck deep into the very pith; the tree fell to the earth with a sigh: he felt a pang—it was like a swoon; he could not think of happiness, for he was sorrowful at being separated from his home, from the place where he had sprung up. He well knew that he should never see his dear old comrades, the little bushes and flowers around him, any more; perhaps not even the birds! The departure was not at all agreeable.

The Tree only came to himself when he was unloaded in a courtyard with the other trees, and heard a man say, "That one is splendid! we don't want the others." Then two servants came in rich livery and carried the Fir Tree into a large and splendid drawing room. Portraits were hanging on the walls, and near the white porcelain stove stood two large Chinese vases with lions on the covers. There, too, were large easy chairs, silken sofas, large tables full of picture books, and full of toys worth hundreds and hundreds of crowns—at least the children said so. And the Fir Tree was stuck upright in a cask that was filled with sand: but no one could see that it was a cask, for green cloth was hung all round it, and it stood on a large gayly colored carpet. O, how the tree quivered! What was to happen? The servants, as well as the young ladies, decorated it. On one branch there hung little nets cut out of colored paper, and each net was filled with sugarplums; and among the other boughs gilded apples and walnuts were suspended, looking as though they had grown there, and little blue and white tapers were placed among the leaves. Dolls that looked for all the world like men—the Tree had never beheld such before—were seen among the foliage, and at the very top a large star of gold tinsel was fixed. It was really splendid—splendid beyond description.

"This evening!" said they all; "how it will shine this evening!"

"O," thought the Tree, "if the evening were but here! If the tapers were but lighted! And then I wonder what will happen! Perhaps the other trees from the forest will come to look at me! Perhaps the sparrows will beat against the window panes! I wonder if I shall take root here, and winter and summer stand covered with ornaments!"

He knew very much about the matter! but he was so impatient that for sheer longing he got a pain in his back, and this with trees is the same thing as a headache with us.

The candles were now lighted. What brightness! What splendor! The Tree trembled so in every bough that one of the tapers set fire to the foliage. It blazed up splendidly.

"Help! help!" cried the young ladies, and they quickly put out the fire.

Now the Tree did not even dare tremble. What a state he was in! He was so uneasy lest he should lose something of his splendor, that he was quite bewildered amidst the glare and brightness; when suddenly both folding doors opened, and a troop of children rushed in as if they would upset the Tree. The older persons followed quietly; the little ones stood quite still. But it was only for a moment; then they shouted so that the whole place re-echoed with their rejoicing; they danced round the Tree, and one present after the other was pulled off.

"What are they about?" thought the Tree. "What is to happen now!" And the lights burned down to the very branches, and as they burned down they were put out one after the other, and then the children had permission to plunder the Tree. So they fell upon it with such violence that all its branches cracked; if it had not been fixed firmly in the cask, it would certainly have tumbled down.

The children danced about with their beautiful playthings; no one looked at the Tree except the old nurse, who peeped between the branches; but it was only to see if there was a fig or an apple left that had been forgotten.

"A story! a story!" cried the children, drawing a little fat man towards the Tree. He seated himself under it, and said, "Now we are in the shade, and the Tree can listen too. But I shall tell only one story. Now which will you have; that about Ivedy-Avedy, or about Klumpy-Dumpy who tumbled downstairs, and yet after all came to the throne and married the princess?"

"Ivedy-Avedy," cried some; "Klumpy-Dumpy," cried the others. There was such a bawling and screaming!—the Fir Tree alone was silent, and he thought to himself, "Am I not to bawl with the rest?—am I to do nothing whatever?" for he was one of the company, and had done what he had to do.

And the man told about Klumpy-Dumpy that tumbled down, who notwithstanding came to the throne, and at last married the princess. And the children clapped their hands, and cried out, "O, go on! Do go on!" They wanted to hear about Ivedy-Avedy too, but the little man only told them about Klumpy-Dumpy. The Fir Tree stood quite still and absorbed in thought: the birds in the wood had never related the like of this. "Klumpy-Dumpy fell downstairs, and yet he married the princess! Yes, yes! that's the way of the world!" thought the Fir Tree, and believed it all, because the man who told the story was so good-looking. "Well, well! who knows, perhaps I may fall downstairs too, and get a princess as wife!" And he looked forward with joy to the morrow, when he hoped to be decked out again with lights, playthings, fruits, and tinsel.

"I won't tremble tomorrow!" thought the Fir Tree. "I will enjoy to the full all my splendor! Tomorrow I shall hear again the story of Klumpy-Dumpy, and perhaps that of Ivedy-Avedy too." And the whole night the Tree stood still and in deep thought.

In the morning the servant and the housemaid came in.

"Now then the splendor will begin again," thought the Fir. But they dragged him out of the room, and up the stairs into the loft; and here in a dark corner, where no daylight could enter, they left him. "What's the meaning of this?" thought the Tree. "What am I to do here? What shall I hear now, I wonder?" And he leaned against the wall lost in reverie. Time enough had he too for his reflections; for days and nights passed on, and nobody came up; and when at last somebody did come, it was only to put some great trunks in a corner out of the way. There stood the Tree quite hidden; it seemed as if he had been entirely forgotten.

" 'Tis now winter out of doors!" thought the Tree. "The earth is hard and covered with snow; men cannot plant me now, and therefore I have been put up here under shelter till the springtime comes! How thoughtful that is! How kind man is, after all! If it only were not so dark here, and so terribly lonely! Not even a hare. And out in the woods it was so pleasant, when the snow was on the ground, and the hare leaped by; yes—even when he jumped over me; but I did not like it then. It is really terribly lonely here!"

"Squeak! squeak!" said a little mouse at the same moment, peeping out of his hole. And then another little one came. They snuffed about the Fir Tree, and rustled among the branches.

"It is dreadfully cold," said the mouse. "But for that, it would be delightful here, old Fir, wouldn't it?"

"I am by no means old," said the Fir Tree. "There's many a one considerably older than I am."

"Where do you come from," asked the mice; "and what can you do?"

They were so extremely curious. "Tell us about the most beautiful spot on the earth. Have you never been there? Were you never in the larder, where cheeses lie on the shelves, and hams hang from above; where one dances about on tallow candles; that place where one enters lean, and comes out again fat and portly?"

"I know no such place," said the Tree. "But I know the wood, where the sun shines, and where the little birds sing." And then he told all about his youth; and the little mice had never heard the like before; and they listened and said—

"Well, to be sure! How much you have seen! How happy you must have been!"

"I!" said the Fir Tree, thinking over what he had himself related. "Yes, in reality those were happy times." And then he told about Christmas Eve, when he was decked out with cakes and candles.

"O," said the little mice, "how fortunate you have been, old Fir Tree!"

"I am by no means old," said he. "I came from the wood this winter; I am in my prime, and am only rather short for my age."

"What delightful stories you know!" said the mice: and the next night they came with four other little mice, who were to hear what the Tree recounted; and the more he related, the more plainly he remembered all himself; and it appeared as if those times had really been happy times. "But they may still come—they may still come. Klumpy-Dumpy fell downstairs, and yet he got a princess!" and he thought at the moment of a nice little birch tree growing out in the woods: to the Fir, that would be a real charming princess.

"Who is Klumpy-Dumpy?" asked the mice. So then the Fir Tree told the whole fairy tale, for he could remember every single word of it; and the little mice jumped for joy up to the very top of the Tree. Next night two more mice came, and on Sunday two rats, even; but they said the stories were not interesting, which vexed the little mice; and they, too, now began to think them not so very amusing either.

"Do you know only one story?" asked the rats.

"Only that one," answered the Tree. "I heard it on my happiest evening; but I did not then know how happy I was."

"It is a very stupid story! Don't you know one about bacon and tallow candles? Can't you tell any larder stories?"

"No," said the Tree.

"Then good-by," said the rats; and they went home.

At last the little mice stayed away also; and the Tree sighed: "After all, it was very pleasant when the sleek little mice sat round me and listened to what I told them. Now that too is over. But I will take good care to enjoy myself when I am brought out again."

But when was that to be? Why, one morning there came a quantity of people and set to work in the loft. The trunks were moved, the tree was pulled out and thrown—rather hard, it is true—down on the floor, but a man drew him towards the stairs, where the daylight shone.

"Now a merry life will begin again," thought the Tree. He felt the fresh air, the first sunbeam—and now he was out in the courtyard. All passed so quickly, there was so much going on around him, that the Tree quite forgot to look to himself. The court adjoined a garden, and all was in flower; the roses hung so fresh and odorous over the balustrade, the lindens were in blossom, the swallows flew by, and said "Quirre-vit! my husband is come!" but it was not the Fir Tree that they meant.

"Now, then, I shall really enjoy life," said he, exultingly, and spread out his branches; but, alas! they were all withered and yellow. It was in a corner that he lay, among weeds and nettles. The golden star of tinsel was still on the top of the Tree, and glittered in the sunshine.

In the courtyard some of the merry children were playing who had danced at Christmas round the Fir Tree, and were so glad at the sight of him. One of the youngest ran and tore off the golden star.

"Only look what is still on the ugly old Christmas tree!" said he, trampling on the branches, so that they all cracked beneath his feet.

And the Tree beheld all the beauty of the flowers, and the freshness in the garden; he beheld himself, and wished he had remained in his dark corner in the loft: he thought of his first youth in the wood, of the merry Christmas Eve, and of the little mice who had listened with so much pleasure to the story of Klumpy-Dumpy.

"It's over—it's past!" said the poor Tree. "Had I but rejoiced when I had reason to do so! But now it's past, it's past!"

And the gardener's boy chopped the Tree into small pieces;

there was a whole heap lying there. The wood flamed up splendidly under the large brewing copper, and it sighed so deeply! Each sigh was like a shot.

The boys played about in the court, and the youngest wore the gold star on his breast which the Tree had had on the happiest evening of his life. However, that was over now—the Tree gone, the story at an end.

The Adventure of the Blue Carbuncle

Sir Arthur Conan Doyle

I had called upon my friend Sherlock Holmes upon the second morning after Christmas, with the intention of wishing him the compliments of the season. He was lounging upon the sofa in a purple dressing-gown, a pipe-rack within his reach upon the right, and a pile of crumpled morning papers, evidently newly studied, near at hand. Beside the couch was a wooden chair, and on the angle of the back hung a very seedy and disreputable hard-felt hat, much the worse for wear, and cracked in several places. A lens and a forceps lying upon the seat of the chair suggested that the hat had been suspended in this manner for the purpose of examination.

"You are engaged," said I; "perhaps I interrupt you."

"Not at all. I am glad to have a friend with whom I can discuss my results. The matter is a perfectly trivial one"—he jerked his thumb in the direction of the old hat—"but there are points in connection with it which are not entirely devoid of interest and even of instruction."

I seated myself in his armchair and warmed my hands before his crackling fire, for a sharp frost had set in, and the windows were thick with the ice crystals. "I suppose," I remarked, "that, homely as it looks, this thing has some deadly story linked on to it—that it is the clue which will guide you in the solution of some mystery and the punishment of some crime."

"No, no. No crime," said Sherlock Holmes, laughing. "Only one of those whimsical little incidents which will happen when you have four million human beings all jostling each other within the space of a few square miles. Amid the action and reaction of so dense a swarm of humanity, every possible combination of events may be expected to take place, and many a little problem will be presented which may be striking and bizarre without being criminal. We have already had experience of such."

"So much so," I remarked, "that of the last six cases which I have added to my notes, three have been entirely free of any legal crime."

"Precisely. You allude to my attempt to recover the Irene Adler papers, to the singular case of Miss Mary Sutherland, and to the adventure of the man with the twisted lip. Well, I have no doubt that this small matter will fall into the same innocent category. You know Peterson, the commissionaire?"

"Yes."

"It is to him that this trophy belongs."

"It is his hat."

"No, no; he found it. Its owner is unknown. I beg that you will look upon it not as a battered billycock but as an intellectual problem. And, first, as to how it came here. It arrived upon Christmas morning, in company with a good fat goose, which is, I have no doubt, roasting at this moment in front of Peterson's fire. The facts are these: about four o'clock on Christmas morning, Peterson, who, as you know, is a very honest fellow, was returning from small small jollification and was making his way homeward down Tottenham Court Road. In front of him he saw, in the gaslight, a tallish man, walking with a slight stagger, and carrying a white goose slung over his shoulder. As he reached the corner of Goodge Street, a row broke out between this stranger and a little knot of roughs. One of the latter knocked off the man's hat, on which he raised his stick to defend himself and, swinging it over his head, smashed the shop window behind him. Peterson had rushed forward to protect the stranger from his assailants; but the man, shocked at having broken the window, and seeing an official-looking person in uniform rushing towards him, dropped his goose, took to his heels, and vanished amid the labyrinth of small streets which lie at the back of Tottenham Court Road. The roughs had also fled at the appearance of Peterson, so that he was left in possession of the field of battle, and also of the spoils of victory in the shape of this battered hat and a most unimpeachable Christmas goose."

"Which surely he restored to their owner?"

"My dear fellow, there lies the problems. It is true that 'For Mrs. Henry Baker' was printed upon a small card which was tied to the bird's left leg, and it is also true that the initials 'H. B.' are legible upon the lining of this hat; but as there are some thousands of Bakers, and some hundreds of Henry Bakers in this city of ours, it is not easy to restore lost property to any one of them."

"What, then, did Peterson do?"

"He brought round both hat and goose to me on Christmas morning, knowing that even the smallest problems are of interest to me. The goose we retained until this morning, when there were signs that, in spite of the slight frost, it would be well that it should be eaten without unnecessary delay. Its finder has carried it off, therefore, to fulfil the ultimate destiny of a goose, while I continue to retain the hat of the unknown gentleman who lost his Christmas dinner."

"Did he not advertise?"

"No."

"Then, what clue could you have as to his identity?"

"Only as much as we can deduce."

"From his hat?"

"Precisely."

"But you are joking. What can you gather from this old battered felt?"

"Here is my lens. You know my methods. What can you gather yourself as to the individuality of the man who has worn this article?"

I took the tattered object in my hands and turned it over rather ruefully. It was a very ordinary black hat of the usual round shape, hard and much the worse for wear. The lining had been of red silk, but was a good deal discoloured. There was no maker's name; but, as Holmes had remarked, the initials "H. B." were scrawled upon one side. It was pierced in the brim for a hat-securer, but the elastic was missing. For the rest, it was cracked, exceedingly dusty, and spotted in several places, although there seemed to have been some attempt to hide the discoloured patches by smearing them with ink.

"I can see nothing," said I, handing it back to my friend.

"On the contrary, Watson, you can see everything. You fail, however, to reason from what you see. You are too timid in drawing your inferences."

"Then, pray tell me what it is that you can infer from this hat?"

He picked it up and gazed at it in the peculiar introspective fashion which was characteristic of him. "It is perhaps less suggestive than it might have been," he remarked, "and yet there are a few inferences which are very distinct, and a few others which represent at least a strong balance of probability. That the man was highly intellectual is of course obvious upon the face of it, and also that he was fairly well-to-do within the last three years, although he has now fallen upon evil days. He had foresight, but has less now than formerly, pointing to a moral retrogression, which, when taken with the decline of his fortunes, seems to indicate some evil influence, probably drink, at work upon him. This may account also for the obvious fact that his wife has ceased to love him."

"My dear Holmes!"

"He has, however, retained some degree of self-respect," he continued, disregarding my remonstrance. "He is a man who leads a sedentary life, goes out little, is out of training entirely, is middle-aged, has grizzled hair which he has had cut within the last few days, and which he anoints with lime-cream. These are the more patent facts which are to be deduced from his hat. Also, by the way, that it is extremely improbable that he has gas laid on in his house."

"You are certainly joking, Holmes."

"Not in the least. Is it possible that even now, when I give you these results, you are unable to see how they are attained?"

"I have no doubt that I am very stupid, but I must confess that I am unable to follow you. For example, how did you deduce that this man was intellectual?"

For answer Holmes clapped the hat upon his head. It came right over the forehead and settled upon the bridge of his nose. "It is a question of cubic capacity," said he; "a man with so large a brain must have something in it."

"The decline of his fortunes, then?"

"This hat is three years old. These flat brims curled at the edge came in then. It is a hat of the very best quality. Look at the band of ribbed silk and the excellent lining. If this man could afford to buy so expensive a hat three years ago, and has had no hat since, then he has assuredly gone down in the world."

"Well, that is clear enough, certainly. But how about the foresight and the moral retrogression?"

Sherlock Holmes laughed. "Here is the foresight," said he, putting his finger upon the little disc and loop of the hat-securer. "They are never sold upon hats. If this man ordered one, it is a sign of a certain amount of foresight, since he went out of his way to take this precaution against the wind. But since we see that he has broken the elastic and has not troubled to replace it, it is obvious that he has less foresight now than formerly, which is a distinct proof of a weakening nature. On the other hand, he has endeavoured to conceal some of these stains upon the felt by daubing them with ink, which is a sign that he has not entirely lost his self-respect."

"Your reasoning is certainly plausible."

"The further points, that he is middle-aged, that his hair is grizzled, that it has been recently cut, and that he uses lime-cream, are all to be gathered from a close examination of the lower part of the lining. The lens discloses a large number of hair-ends, clean cut by the scissors of the barber. They all appear to be adhesive, and there is a distinct odour of lime-cream. This dust, you will observe, is not the gritty, gray dust of the street but the fluffy brown dust of the house, showing that it has been hung up indoors most of the time; while the marks of moisture upon the inside are proof positive that the wearer perspired very freely, and could, therefore, hardly be in the best of training."

"But his wife—you said that she had ceased to love him."

"This hat has not been brushed for weeks. When I see you, my dear Watson, with a week's accumulation of dust upon your hat, and when your wife allows you to go out in such a state, I shall fear that you also have been unfortunate enough to lose your wife's affection."

"But he might be a bachelor."

"Nay, he was bringing home the goose as a peace-offering to his wife. Remember the card upon the bird's leg."

"You have an answer to everything. But how on earth do you deduce that the gas is not laid on in his house?"

"One tallow stain, or even two, might come by chance; but when I see no less than five, I think that there can be little doubt that the individual must be brought into frequent contact with burning tallow—walks upstairs at night probably with his hat in one hand and a guttering candle in the other. Anyhow, he never got tallow-stains from a gas-jet. Are you satisfied?"

"Well, it is very ingenious," said I, laughing; "but since, as you said just now, there has been no crime committed, and no harm done save the loss of a goose, all this seems to be rather a waste of energy."

Sherlock Holmes had opened his mouth to reply, when the door flew open, and Peterson, the commissionaire, rushed into the apartment with flushed cheeks and the face of a man who is dazed with astonishment.

"The goose, Mr. Holmes! The goose, sir!" he gasped.

"Eh? What of it, then? Has it returned to life and flapped off through the kitchen window?" Holmes twisted himself round upon the sofa to get a fairer view of the man's excited face.

"See here, sir! See what my wife found in its crop!" He held out his hand and displayed upon the centre of the palm a brilliantly scintillating blue stone, rather smaller than a bean in size, but of such purity and radiance that it twinkled like an electric point in the dark hollow of his hand.

Sherlock Holmes sat up with a whistle. "By Jove, Peterson!" said he, "this is treasure trove indeed. I suppose you know what you have got?"

"A diamond, sir? A precious stone. It cuts into glass as though it were putty."

"It's more than a precious stone. It is *the* precious stone."

"Not the Countess of Morcar's blue carbuncle!" I ejaculated.

"Precisely so. I ought to know its size and shape, seeing that I have read the advertisement about it in *The Times* every day lately. It is absolutely unique, and its value can only be conjectured, but the reward offered of £1000 is certainly not within a twentieth part of the market price."

"A thousand pounds! Great Lord of mercy!" The commissionaire plumped down into a chair and stared from one to the other of us.

"That is the reward, and I have reason to know that there are sentimental considerations in the background which would induce the Countess to part with half her fortune if she could but recover the gem."

"It was lost, if I remember aright, at the Hotel Cosmopolitan," I remarked.

"Precisely so, on December 22d, just five days ago. John Horner, a plumber, was accused of having abstracted it from the lady's jewel-case. The evidence against him was so strong that the case has been referred to the Assizes. I have some account of the matter here, I believe." He rummaged amid his newspapers, glancing over the dates, until at last he smoothed one out, doubled it over, and read the following paragraph:

> Hotel Cosmopolitan Jewel Robbery. John Horner, 26, plumber, was brought up upon the charge of having upon the 22nd inst. abstracted from the jewel-case of the Countess of Morcar the valuable gem known as the blue carbuncle. James Ryder, upper-attendant at the hotel, gave his evidence to the effect that he had shown Horner up to the dressing-room of the Countess of Morcar upon the day of the robbery in order that he might solder the second bar of the grate, which was loose. He had remained with Horner some little time, but had finally been called away. On returning, he found that Horner had disappeared, that the bureau had been forced open, and that the small morocco casket in which, as it afterwards transpired, the Countess was accustomed to keep her jewel, was lying empty upon the dressing-table. Ryder instantly gave the alarm, and Horner was arrested the same evening; but the stone could not be found either upon his person or in his rooms. Catherine Cusack, maid to the Countess, deposed to having heard Ryder's cry of dismay on discovering the robbery, and to having rushed into the room, where she found matters as described by the last witness. Inspector Bradstreet, B division, gave evidence as to the arrest of Horner, who struggled frantically, and protested his innocence in the strongest terms. Evidence of a previous conviction for robbery having been given against the prisoner, the magistrate refused to deal summarily with the offence, but referred it to the Assizes. Horner, who had shown signs of intense emotion during the proceedings, fainted away at the conclusion and was carried out of court.

"Hum! So much for the police-court," said Holmes thoughtfully, tossing aside the paper. "The question for us now to solve is the sequence of events leading from a rifled jewel-case at one end to the crop of a goose in Tottenham Court Road at the other. You see, Watson, our little deductions have suddenly assumed a much more important and less innocent aspect. Here is the stone; the stone came from the goose, and the goose came from Mr. Henry Baker, the gentleman with the bad hat and all the other characteristics with which I have bored you. So now we must set ourselves very seriously to finding this gentleman and ascertaining what part he has played in this little mystery. To do this, we must try the simplest means first, and these lie undoubtedly in an advertisement in all the evening papers. If this fail, I shall have recourse to other methods."

"What will you say?"

"Give me a pencil and that slip of paper. Now, then:

> Found at the corner of Goodge Street, a goose and a black felt hat. Mr. Henry Baker can have the same by applying at 6:30 this evening at 221B, Baker Street.

That is clear and concise."

"Very. But will he see it?"

"Well, he is sure to keep an eye on the papers, since, to a poor man, the loss was a heavy one. He was clearly so scared by his mischance in breaking the window and by the approach of Peterson that he thought of nothing but flight, but since then he must have bitterly regretted the impulse which caused him to drop his bird. Then, again, the introduction of his name will cause him to see it, for everyone who knows him will direct his attention to it. Here you are, Peterson, run down to the advertising agency and have this put in the evening papers."

"In which, sir?"

"Oh, in the *Globe, Star, Pall Mall, St. James's, Evening News Standard, Echo,* and any others that occur to you."

"Very well, sir. And this stone?"

"Ah, yes, I shall keep the stone. Thank you. And, I say, Peterson, just buy a goose on your way back and leave it here with me, for we must have one to give to this gentleman in place of the one which your family is now devouring."

When the commissionaire had gone, Holmes took up the stone and held it against the light. "It's a bonny thing," said he. "Just see how it glints and sparkles. Of course it is a nucleus and focus of crime. Every good stone is. They are the devil's pet baits. In the larger and older jewels every facet may stand for a bloody deed. This stone is not yet twenty years old. It was found in the banks of the Amoy River in southern China and is remarkable in having every characteristic of the carbuncle, save that it is blue in shade instead of ruby red. In spite of its youth, it has already a sinister history. There have been two murders, a vitriol-throwing, a suicide, and several robberies brought about for the sake of this forty-grain weight of crystallized charcoal. Who would think that so pretty a toy would be a purveyor to the gallows and the prison? I'll lock it up in my strong box now and drop a line to the Countess to say that we have it."

"Do you think that this man Horner is innocent?"

"I cannot tell."

"Well, then, do you imagine that this other one, Henry Baker, had anything to do with the matter?"

"It is, I think, much more likely that Henry Baker is an absolutely innocent man, who had no idea that the bird which he was carrying was of considerably more value than if it were made of solid gold. That, however, I shall determine by a very simple test if we have an answer to our advertisement."

"And you can do nothing until then?"

"Nothing."

"In that case I shall continue my professional round. But I shall come back in the evening at the hour you have mentioned, for I should like to see the solution of so tangled a business."

"Very glad to see you. I dine at seven. There is a woodcock, I believe. By the way, in view of recent occurrences, perhaps I ought to ask Mrs. Hudson to examine its crop."

I had been delayed at a case, and it was a little after half-past six when I found myself in Baker Street once more. As I approached the house I saw a tall man in a Scotch bonnet with a coat which was buttoned up to his chin waiting outside in the bright semicircle which was thrown from the fanlight. Just as I arrived the door was opened, and we were shown up together to Holmes's room.

"Mr. Henry Baker, I believe," said he, rising from his armchair and greeting his visitor with the easy air of geniality which he could so readily assume. "Pray take this chair by the fire, Mr. Baker. It is a cold night, and I observe that your circulation is more adapted for summer than for winter. Ah, Watson, you have just come at the right time. Is that your hat, Mr. Baker?"

"Yes, sir, that is undoubtedly my hat."

He was a large man with rounded shoulders, a massive head, and a broad, intelligent face, sloping down to a pointed beard of grizzled brown. A touch of red in nose and cheeks, with a slight tremor of his extended hand, recalled Holmes's surmise as to his habits. His rusty black frock-coat was buttoned right up in front, with the collar turned up, and his lank wrists protruded from his sleeves without a sign of cuff or shirt. He spoke in a slow staccato fashion, choosing his words with care, and gave the impression generally of a man of learning and letters who had had ill-usage at the hands of fortune.

"We have retained these things for some days," said Holmes, "because we expected to see an advertisement from you giving your address. I am at a loss to know now why you did not advertise."

Our visitor gave a rather shamefaced laugh. "Shillings have not been so plentiful with me as they once were," he remarked. "I had no doubt that the gang of roughs who assaulted me had carried off both my hat and the bird. I did not care to spend more money in a hopeless attempt at recovering them."

"Very naturally. By the way, about the bird, we were compelled to eat it."

"To eat it!" Our visitor half rose from his chair in his excitement.

"Yes, it would have been of no use to anyone had we not done so. But I presume that this other goose upon the sideboard, which is about the same weight and perfectly fresh, will answer your purpose equally well?"

"Oh, certainly, certainly," answered Mr. Baker with a sigh of relief.

"Of course, we still have the feathers, legs, crop, and so on of your own bird, so if you wish——"

The man burst into a hearty laugh. "They might be useful to me as relics of my adventure," said he, "but beyond that I can hardly see what use the *disjecta membra* of my late acquaintance are going to be to me. No, sir, I think that, with your permission, I will confine my attentions to the excellent bird which I perceive upon the sideboard."

Sherlock Holmes glanced sharply across at me with a slight shrug of his shoulders.

"There is your hat, then, and there your bird," said he. "By the way, would it bore you to tell me where you got the other one from? I am somewhat of a fowl fancier, and I have seldom seen a better-grown goose."

"Certainly, sir," said Baker, who had risen and tucked his newly gained property under his arm. "There are a few of us who frequent the Alpha Inn, near the Museum—we are to be found in the Museum itself during the day, you understand. This year our good host, Windigate by name, instituted a goose club, by which, on consideration of some few pence every week, we were each to receive a bird at Christmas. My pence were duly paid, and the rest is familiar to you. I am much indebted to you, sir, for a Scotch bonnet is fitted neither to my years nor my gravity." With a comical pomposity of manner he bowed solemnly to both of us and strode off upon his way.

"So much for Mr. Henry Baker," said Holmes when he had closed the door behind him. "It is quite certain that he knows nothing whatever about the matter. Are you hungry, Watson?"

"Not particularly."

"Then I suggest that we turn our dinner into a supper and follow up this clue while it is still hot."

"By all means."

It was a bitter night, so we drew on our ulsters and wrapped cravats about our throats. Outside, the stars were shining coldly in a cloudless sky, and the breath of the passers-by blew out into smoke like so many pistol shots. Our footfalls rang out crisply and loudly as we swung through the doctors' quarter, Wimpole Street, Harley Street, and so through Wigmore Street into Oxford street. In a quarter of an hour we were in Bloomsbury at the Alpha Inn, which is a small public-house at the corner of one of the streets which runs down into Holborn. Holmes pushed open the door of the private bar and ordered two glasses of beer from the ruddy-faced, white-aproned landlord.

"Your beer should be excellent if it is as good as your geese," said he.

"My geese!" The man seemed surprised.

"Yes. I was speaking only half an hour ago to Mr. Henry Baker, who was a member of your goose club."

"Ah! yes, I see. But you see, sir, them's not *our* geese."

"Indeed! Whose, then?"

"Well, I got the two dozen from a salesman in Covent Garden."

"Indeed? I know some of them. Which was it?"

"Breckinridge is his name."

"Ah! I don't know him. Well, here's your good health, landlord, and prosperity to your house. Good-night.

"Now for Mr. Breckinridge," he continued, buttoning up his coat as we came out into the frosty air. "Remember, Watson, that though we have so homely a thing as a goose at one end of this chain, we have at the other a man who will certainly get seven years' penal servitude unless we can establish his innocence. It is possible that our inquiry may but confirm his guilt; but, in any case, we have a line of investigation which has been missed by the police, and which a singular chance has placed in our hands. Let us follow it out to the bitter end. Faces to the south, then, and quick march!"

We passed across Holborn, down Endell Street, and so through a zigzag of slums to Covent Garden Market. One of the largest stalls bore the name of Breckinridge upon it, and the proprietor, a horsy-looking man, with a sharp face and trim side-whiskers, was helping a boy to put up the shutters.

"Good-evening. It's a cold night," said Holmes.

The salesman nodded and shot a questioning glance at my companion.

"Sold out of geese, I see," continued Holmes, pointing at the bare slabs of marble.

"Let you have five hundred tomorrow morning."

"That's no good."

"Well, there are some on the stall with the gas-flare."

"Ah, but I was recommended to you."

"Who by?"

"The landlord of the Alpha."

"Oh, yes; I sent him a couple of dozen."

"Fine birds they were, too. Now where did you get them from?"

To my surprise the question provoked a burst of anger from the salesman.

"Now, then, mister," said he, with his head cocked and his arms akimbo, "what are you driving at? Let's have it straight, now."

"It is straight enough. I should like to know who sold you the geese which you supplied to the Alpha."

"Well, then, I shan't tell you. So now!"

"Oh, it is a matter of no importance; but I don't know why you should be so warm over such a trifle."

"Warm! You'd be as warm, maybe, if you were as pestered as I am. When I pay good money for a good article there should be an end of the business; but it's 'Where are the geese?' and 'Who did you sell the geese to?' and 'What will you take for the geese?' One would think they were the only geese in the world, to hear the fuss that is made over them."

"Well, I have no connection with any other people who have been making inquiries," said Holmes carelessly. "If you won't tell us the bet is off, that is all. But I'm always ready to back my opinion on a matter of fowls, and I have a fiver on it that the bird I ate is country bred."

"Well, then, you've lost your fiver, for it's town bred," snapped the salesman.

"It's nothing of the kind."

"I say it is."

"I don't believe it."

"D'you think you know more about fowls than I, who have handled them ever since I was a nipper? I tell you, all those birds that went to the Alpha were town bred."

"You'll never persuade me to believe that."

"Will you bet, then?"

"It's merely taking your money, for I know that I am right. But I'll have a sovereign on with you, just to teach you not to be obstinate."

The salesman chuckled grimly. "Bring me the books, Bill," said he.

The small boy brought round a small thin volume and a great greasy-backed one, laying them out together beneath the hanging lamp.

"Now then, Mr. Cocksure," said the salesman, "I thought that I was out of geese, but before I finish you'll find that there is still one left in my shop. You see this little book?"

"Well?"

"That's the list of the folk from whom I buy. D'you see? Well, then, here on this page are the country folk, and the numbers after their names are where their accounts are in the big ledger. Now, then! You see this other page in red ink? Well, that is a list of my town suppliers. Now, look at that third name. Just read it out to me."

" 'Mrs. Oakshott, 117, Brixton Road—249,' " read Holmes.

"Quite so. Now turn that up in the ledger."

Holmes turned to the page indicated. "Here you are, 'Mrs. Oakshott, 117, Brixton Road, egg and poultry supplier.' "

"Now, then, what's the last entry?"

" 'December 22d. Twenty-four geese at 7*s.* 6*d.*' "

"Quite so. There you are. And underneath?"

" 'Sold to Mr. Windigate of the Alpha, at 12*s.*' "

"What have you to say now?"

Sherlock Holmes looked deeply chagrined. He drew a sovereign from his pocket and threw it down upon the slab, turning away with the air of a man whose disgust is too deep for words. A few yards off he stopped under a lamp-post and laughed in the hearty, noiseless fashion which was peculiar to him.

"When you see a man with whiskers of that cut and the 'pink 'un' protruding out of his pocket, you can always draw him by a bet," said he. "I daresay that if I had put £100 down in front of him, that man would not have given me such complete information as was drawn from him by the idea that he was doing me on a wager. Well, Watson, we are, I fancy, nearing the end of our quest, and the only point which remains to be determined is whether we should go on to this Mrs. Oakshott tonight, or whether we should reserve it for tomorrow. It is clear from what that surly fellow said that there are others besides ourselves who are anxious about the matter, and I should——"

His remarks were suddenly cut short by a loud hubbub which broke out from the stall which we had just left. Turning round we saw a little rat-faced fellow standing in the centre of the circle of yellow light which was thrown by the swinging lamp, while Breckinridge the salesman, framed in the door of his stall, was shaking his fists fiercely at the cringing figure.

"I've had enough of you and your geese," he shouted. "I wish you were all at the devil together. If you come pestering me any more with your silly talk I'll set the dog at you. You bring Mrs. Oakshott here and I'll answer her, but what have you to do with it? Did I buy the geese off you?"

"No; but one of them was mine all the same," whined the little man.

"Well, then, ask Mrs. Oakshott for it."

"She told me to ask you."

"Well, you can ask the King of Proosia, for all I care. I've had enough of it. Get out of this!" He rushed fiercely forward, and the inquirer flitted away into the darkness.

"Ha! this may save us a visit to Brixton Road," whispered Holmes. "Come with me, and we will see what is to be made of this fellow." Striding through the scattered knots of people who lounged round the flaring stalls, my companion speedily overtook the little man and touched him upon the shoulder. He sprang round, and I could see in the gas-light that every vestige of colour had been driven from his face.

"Who are you, then? What do you want?" he asked in a quavering voice.

"You will excuse me," said Holmes blandly, "but I could not help overhearing the questions which you put to the salesman just now. I think that I could be of assistance to you."

"You? Who are you? How could you know anything of the matter?"

"My name is Sherlock Holmes. It is my business to know what other people don't know."

"But you can know nothing of this?"

"Excuse me, I know everything of it. You are endeavouring to trace some geese which were sold by Mrs. Oakshott, of Brixton Road, to a salesman named Breckinridge, by him in turn to Mr. Windigate, of the Alpha, and by him to his club, of which Mr. Henry Baker is a member."

"Oh, sir, you are the very man whom I have longed to meet,"

cried the little fellow with outstretched hands and quivering fingers. "I can hardly explain to you how interested I am in this matter."

Sherlock Holmes hailed a four-wheeler which was passing. "In that case we had better discuss it in a cosy room rather than in this wind-swept market-place," said he. "But pray tell me, before we go farther, who it is that I have the pleasure of assisting."

The man hesitated for an instant. "My name is John Robinson," he answered with a sidelong glance.

"No, no; the real name," said Holmes sweetly. "It is always awkward doing business with an alias."

A flush sprang to the white cheeks of the stranger. "Well, then," said he, "my real name is James Ryder."

"Precisely so. Head attendant at the Hotel Cosmopolitan. Pray step into the cab, and I shall soon be able to tell you everything which you would wish to know."

The little man stood glancing from one to the other of us with half-frightened, half-hopeful eyes, as one who is not sure whether he is on the verge of a windfall or of a catastrophe. Then he stepped into the cab, and in half an hour we were back in the sitting-room at Baker Street. Nothing had been said during our drive, but the high, thin breathing of our new companion, and the claspings and unclaspings of his hands, spoke of the nervous tension within him.

"Here we are!" said Holmes cheerily as we filed into the room. "The fire looks very seasonable in this weather. You look cold, Mr. Ryder. Pray take the basket-chair. I will just put on my slippers before we settle this little matter of yours. Now, then! You want to know what became of those geese?"

"Yes, sir."

"Or rather, I fancy, of that goose. It was one bird, I imagine, in which you were interested—white, with a black bar across the tail."

Ryder quivered with emotion. "Oh, sir," he cried, "can you tell me where it went to?"

"It came here."

"Here?"

"Yes, and a most remarkable bird it proved. I don't wonder that you should take an interest in it. It laid an egg after it was dead—the bonniest, brightest little blue egg that ever was seen. I have it here in my museum."

Our visitor staggered to his feet and clutched the mantel-piece with his right hand. Holmes unlocked his strong-box and held up the blue carbuncle, which shone out like a star, with a cold, brilliant, many-pointed radiance. Ryder stood glaring with a drawn face, uncertain whether to claim or to disown it.

"The game's up, Ryder," said Holmes quietly. "Hold up, man, or you'll be into the fire! Give him an arm back into his chair, Watson. He's not got blood enough to go in for felony with impunity. Give him a dash of brandy. So! Now he looks a little more human. What a shrimp it is, to be sure!"

For a moment he had staggered and nearly fallen, but the brandy brought a tinge of colour into his cheeks, and he sat staring with frightened eyes at his accuser.

"I have almost every link in my hands, and all the proofs which I could possibly need, so there is little which you need tell me. Still, that little may as well be cleared up to make the case complete. You had heard, Ryder, of this blue stone of the Countess of Morcar's?"

"It was Catherine Cusack who told me of it," said he in a crackling voice.

"I see—her ladyship's waiting-maid. Well, the temptation of sudden wealth so easily acquired was too much for you, as it has been for better men before you; but you were not very scrupulous in the means you used. It seems to me, Ryder, that there is the making of a very pretty villain in you. You knew that this man Horner, the plumber, had been concerned in some such matter before, and that suspicion would rest the more readily upon him. What did you do, then? You made some small job in my lady's room—you and your confederate Cusack—and you managed that he should be the man sent for. Then, when he had left, you rifled the jewel-case, raised the alarm, and had this unfortunate man arrested. You then——"

Ryder threw himself down suddenly upon the rug and clutched at my companion's knees. "For God's sake, have mercy!" he shrieked. "Think of my father! of my mother! It would break their hearts. I never went wrong before! I never will again. I swear it. I'll swear it on a Bible. Oh, don't bring it into court! For Christ's sake, don't!"

"Get back into your chair!" said Holmes sternly. "It is very well to cringe and crawl now, but you thought little enough of this poor Horner in the dock for a crime of which he knew nothing."

"I will fly, Mr. Holmes. I will leave the country, sir. Then the charge against him will break down."

"Hum! We will talk about that. And now let us hear a true account of the next act. How came the stone into the goose, and how came the goose into the open market? Tell us the truth, for there lies your only hope of safety."

Ryder passed his tongue over his parched lips. "I will tell you it just as it happened, sir," said he. "When Horner had been arrested, it seemed to me that it would be best for me to get away with the stone at once, for I did not know at what moment the police might not take it into their heads to search me and my room. There was no place about the hotel where it would be safe. I went out, as if on some commission, and I made for my sister's house. She had married a man named Oakshott, and lived in Brixton Road, where she fattened fowls for the market. All the way there every man I met seemed to me to be a policeman or a detective; and, for all that it was a cold night, the sweat was pouring down my face before I came to the Brixton Road. My sister asked me what was the matter, and why I was so pale; but I told her that I had been upset by the jewel robbery at the hotel. Then I went into the back yard and smoked a pipe, and wondered what it would be best to do.

"I had a friend once called Maudsley, who went to the bad, and has just been serving his time in Pentonville. One day he had met me, and fell into talk about the ways of thieves, and how they could get rid of what they stole. I knew that he would be true to me, for I knew one or two things about him; so I made up my mind to go right on to Kilburn, where he lived, and take him into my confidence. He would show me how to turn the stone into money. But how to get to him in safety? I thought of the agonies I had gone through in coming from the hotel. I might at any moment be seized and searched, and there would be the stone in my waistcoat pocket. I was leaning against the wall at the time and looking at the geese which were waddling about round my feet, and suddenly an idea came into my head which showed me how I could beat the best detective that ever lived.

"My sister had told me some weeks before that I might have the pick of her geese for a Christmas present, and I knew that she was always as good as her word. I would take my goose now, and in it I would carry my stone to Kilburn. There was a little shed in the yard, and behind this I drove one of the birds—a fine big one, white, with a barred tail. I caught it, and, prying its bill open, I thrust the stone down its throat as far as my finger could reach. The bird gave a gulp, and I felt the stone pass along its gullet and down into its crop. But the creature flapped and struggled, and out came my sister to know what was the matter. As I turned to speak to her the brute broke loose and fluttered off among the others.

" 'Whatever were you doing with that bird, Jem?' says she.

" 'Well," said I, 'you said you'd give me one for Christmas, and I was feeling which was the fattest.'

" 'Oh,' says she, 'we've set yours aside for you—Jem's bird, we call it. It's the big white one over yonder. There's twenty-six of them, which makes one for you, and one for us, and two dozen for the market.'

" 'Thank you, Maggie," says I; 'but if it is all the same to you, I'd rather have that one I was handling just now.'

" 'The other is a good three pound heavier,' said she, 'and we fattened it expressly for you.'

" 'Never mind. I'll have the other, and I'll take it now,' said I.

" 'Oh, just as you like,' said she, a little huffed. 'Which is it you want, then?'

" 'That white one with the barred tail, right in the middle of the flock.'

" 'Oh, very well. Kill it and take it with you.'

"Well, I did what she said, Mr. Holmes, and I carried the bird all the way to Kilburn. I told my pal what I had done, for he was a man that it was easy to tell a thing like that to. He laughed until he choked, and we got a knife and opened the goose. My heart turned to water, for there was no sign of the stone, and I knew that some terrible mistake had occurred. I left the bird, rushed back to my sister's, and hurried into the back yard. There was not a bird to be seen there.

" 'Where are they all, Maggie?' I cried.

" 'Gone to the dealer's, Jem.'

" 'Which dealer's?'

" 'Breckinridge, of Covent Garden.'

" 'But was there another with a barred tail?' I asked 'the same as the one I chose?'

" 'Yes, Jem; there were two barred-tailed ones, and could never tell them apart.'

"Well, then, of course I saw it all, and I ran off as hard as my feet would carry me to this man Breckinridge; but he had sold the lot at once, and not one word would he tell me as to where they had gone. You heard him yourselves tonight. Well, he has always answered me like that. My sister thinks that I am going mad. Sometimes I think that I am myself. And now—and now I am myself a branded thief, without ever having touched the wealth for which I sold my character. God help me! God help me!" He burst into convulsive sobbing, with his face buried in his hands.

There was a long silence, broken only by his heavy breathing, and by the measured tapping of Sherlock Holmes's finger-tips upon the edge of the table. Then my friend rose and threw open the door.

"Get out!" said he.

"What, sir! Oh, Heaven bless you!"

"No more words. Get out!"

And no more words were needed. There was a rush, a clatter upon the stairs, the bang of a door, and the crisp rattle of running footfalls from the street.

"After all, Watson," said Holmes, reaching up his hand for his clay pipe, "I am not retained by the police to supply their deficiencies. If Horner were in danger it would be another thing; but this fellow will not appear against him, and the case must collapse. I suppose that I am commuting a felony, but it is just possible that I am saving a soul. This fellow will not go wrong again; he is too terribly frightened. Send him to jail now, and you make him a jail-bird for life. Besides, it is the season of forgiveness. Chance has put in our way a most singular and whimsical problem, and its solution is its own reward. If you will have the goodness to touch the bell, Doctor, we will begin another investigation, in which, also, a bird will be the chief feature."

POEMS

This selection travels from the Holy Sonnets of John Donne (1572–1631) and John Milton's "On the Morning of Christ's Nativity" (1629) through devotional offerings from Alfred, Lord Tennyson (1809–1892) and Henry Wadsworth Longfellow (1807–1882) to seasonal narratives from the great Scottish storytellers Sir Walter Scott (1771–1832) and Robert Louis Stevenson (1850–1894) and a cosmic verse by Walt Whitman from the Second Annex to Leaves of Grass, *the "death bed" edition of which appeared in 1892. It finishes with Clement Clarke Moore (1779–1863) whose "A Visit from St. Nicholas" was written in 1822.*

Holy Sonnets

John Donne

1

LA CORONA

Deigne *at my hands this crown of prayer and praise,*
Weav'd in my low devout melancholie,
Thou which of good, hast, yea art treasury,
All changing unchang'd Antient of dayes;
But doe not, with a vile crowne of fraile bayes,
Reward my muses white sincerity,
But what thy thorny crowne gain'd, that give mee,
A crowne of Glory, which doth flower alwayes;
The ends crowne our workes, but thou crown'st our ends,
For, at our end begins our endlesse rest;
The first last end, now zealously possest,
With a strong sober thirst, my soule attends.

'Tis time that heart and voice be lifted high,
Salvation to all that will is nigh.

2

ANNUNCIATION

Salvation to all that will is nigh;
That All, which alwayes is All every where,
Which cannot sinne, and yet all sinnes must beare,
Which cannot die, yet cannot chuse but die,
Loe, faithfull Virgin, yeelds himselfe to lye
In prison, in thy wombe; and though he there
Can take no sinne, nor thou give, yet he'will weare
Taken from thence, flesh, which deaths force may trie.
Ere by the spheares time was created, thou
Wast in his minde, who is thy Sonne, and Brother;
Whom thou conceiv'st, conceiv'd; yea thou art now
Thy Makers maker, and thy Fathers mother;
Thou'hast light in darke; and shutst in little roome,
Immensity cloystered in thy deare wombe.

3

NATIVITIE

Immensity cloystered in thy deare wombe,
Now leaves his welbelov'd imprisonment,
There he hath made himselfe to his intent
Weake enough, now into our world to come;
But Oh, for thee, for him, hath th' Inne no roome?
Yet lay him in this stall, and from the Orient,
Starres, and wisemen will travell to prevent

Th'effect of *Herods* jealous generall doome.
Seest thou, my Soule, with thy faiths eyes, how he
Which fils all place, yet none holds him, doth lye?
Was not his pity towards thee wondrous high,
That would have need to be pittied by thee?
Kisse him, and with him into Egypt goe,
With his kinde mother, who partakes thy woe.

4

TEMPLE

With his kinde mother who partakes thy woe,
Joseph turne backe; see where your child doth sit,
Blowing, yea blowing out those sparks of wit,
Which himselfe on the Doctors did bestow;
The Word but lately could not speake, and loe
It sodenly speakes wonders, whence comes it,
That all which was, and all which should be writ,
A shallow seeming child, should deeply know?
His Godhead was not soule to his manhood,
Nor had time mellowed him to this ripenesse,
But as for one which hath a long taske, 'tis good,
With the Sunne to beginne his business,
He in his ages morning thus began
By miracles exceeding power of man.

5

CRUCIFYING

By miracles exceeding power of man,
Hee faith in some, envie in some begat,

For, what weake spirits admire, ambitious, hate;
In both affections many to him ran,
But Oh! the worst are most, they will and can,
Alas, and do, unto the immaculate,
Whose creature Fate is, now prescribe a Fate,
Measuring selfe-lifes infinity to a span,
Nay to an inch. Loe, where condemned hee
Beares his owne crosse, with paine, yet by and by
When it beares him, he must beare more and die.
Now thou art lifted up, draw mee to thee,
And at thy death giving such liberall dole,
Moyst, with one drop of thy blood, my dry soule.

6
RESURRECTION

Moyst with one drop of thy blood, my dry soule
Shall (though she now be in extreme degree
Too stony hard, and yet too fleshly,) bee
Freed by that drop, from being starv'd, hard, or foule,
And life, by this death abled, shall controule
Death, whom thy death slue; nor shall to mee
Feare of first or last death, bring miserie,
If in thy little booke my name thou enroule,
Flesh in that long sleep is not putrified,
But made that there, of which, and for which 'twas;
Nor can by other meanes be glorified.
May then sinnes sleep, and deaths soone from me passe,
That wak't from both, I againe risen may
Salute the last, and everlasting day.

7

ASCENTION

Salute the last and everlasting day,
Joy at the uprising of this Sunne, and Sonne,
Yee whose just teares, or tribulation
Have purely washt, or burnt your drossie clay;
Behold the Highest, parting hence away,
Lightens the darke clouds, which hee treads upon,
Nor doth hee by ascending, show alone,
But first hee, and hee first enters the way.
O strong Ramme, which hast batter'd heaven for mee,
Mild Lambe, which with thy blood, hast mark'd the path;
Bright Torch, which shin'st, that I the way may see,
Oh, with thy owne blood quench thy owne just wrath,
And if thy holy Spirit, my Muse did raise,
Deigne at my hands this crown of prayer and praise.

On the Morning of Christ's Nativity

John Milton

I

This is the month, and this the happy morn,
Wherein the Son of Heaven's eternal King,
Of wedded Maid and Virgin Mother born,
Our great redemption from above did bring;
For so the holy sages once did sing,
    That he our deadly forfeit should release,
And with his Father work us a perpetual peace.

II

That glorious form, that light unsufferable,
And that far-beaming blaze of majesty,
Wherewith he wont at Heaven's high council-table
To sit the midst of Trinal Unity,
He laid aside; and here with us to be,

Forsook the courts of everlasting day,
And chose with us a darksome house of mortal clay.

III

Say, Heavenly Muse, shall not thy sacred vein
Afford a present to the infant God?
Hast thou no verse, no hymn, or solemn strain,
To welcome him to this his new abode,
Now while the Heaven, by the sun's team untrod,
Hath took no print of the approaching light,
And all the spangled host keep watch in squadrons bright?

IV

See how from far upon the eastern road
The star-led wizards haste with odors sweet!
O run, prevent them with thy humble ode,
And lay it lowly at his blessed feet;
Have thou the honor first thy Lord to greet,
And join thy voice unto the angel choir,
From out his secret altar touched with hallowed fire.

THE HYMN

I

It was the winter wild
While the Heaven-born child
All meanly wrapped in the rude manger lies;
Nature in awe to him

Had doffed her gaudy trim,
    With her great Master so to sympathize;
It was no season then for her
To wanton with the sun, her lusty paramour.

II

Only with speeches fair
She woos the gentle air
    To hide her guilty front with innocent snow,
And on her naked shame,
Pollute with sinful blame,
    The saintly veil of maiden white to throw,
Confounded, that her Maker's eyes
Should look so near upon her foul deformities.

III

But he her fears to cease,
Sent down the meek-eyed Peace;
    She, crowned with olive green, came softly sliding
Down through the turning sphere,
His ready harbinger,
    With turtle wing the amorous clouds dividing,
And waving wide her myrtle wand,
She strikes a universal peace through sea and land.

IV

No war or battle's sound
Was heard the world around:
    The idle spear and shield were high uphung;
The hooked chariot stood

Unstained with hostile blood;
    The trumpet spake not to the armed throng;
And kings sat still with awful eye,
As if they surely knew their sovran Lord was by.

V

But peaceful was the night
Wherein the Prince of Light
    His reign of peace upon the earth began:
The winds with wonder whist,
Smoothly the waters kissed,
    Whispering new joys to the mild ocëan,
Who now hath quite forgot to rave,
While birds of calm sit brooding on the charmed wave.

VI

The stars with deep amaze
Stand fixed in steadfast gaze,
    Bending one way their precious influence,
And will not take their flight
For all the morning light,
    Or Lucifer that often warned them thence;
But in their glimmering orbs did glow,
Until their Lord himself bespake, and bid them go.

VII

And though the shady gloom
Had given day her room,
    The sun himself withheld his wonted speed,
And hid his head for shame,

As his inferior flame
    The new-enlightened world no more should need;
He saw a greater sun appear
Than his bright throne or burning axletree could bear.

VIII

The shepherds on the lawn,
Or ere the point of dawn,
    Sat simply chatting in a rustic row;
Full little thought they than
That the mighty Pan
    Was kindly come to live with them below;
Perhaps their loves, or else their sheep,
Was all that did their silly thoughts so busy keep.

IX

When such music sweet
Their hearts and ears did greet,
    As never was by mortal finger strook,
Divinely warbled voice
Answering the stringed noise,
    As all their souls in blissful rapture took;
The air, such pleasure loth to lose,
With thousand echoes still prolongs each heavenly close.

X

Nature that heard such sound
Beneath the hollow round
    Of Cynthia's seat, the airy region thrilling,
Now was almost won

To think her part was done,
    And that her reign had here its last fulfilling;
She knew such harmony alone
Could hold all Heaven and Earth in happier union.

XI

At last surrounds their sight
A globe of circular light,
    That with long beams the shame-faced Night arrayed;
The helmed Cherubim
And sworded Seraphim
    Are seen in glittering ranks with wings displayed,
Harping in loud and solemn choir,
With unexpressive notes to Heaven's new-born Heir.

XII

Such music (as 'tis said)
Before was never made,
    But when of old the sons of morning sung,
While the Creator great
His constellations set,
    And the well-balanced world on hinges hung,
And cast the dark foundations deep,
And bid the weltering waves their oozy channel keep.

XIII

Ring out, ye crystal spheres,
Once bless our human ears
    (If ye have power to touch our senses so),
And let your silver chime

Move in melodious time,
    And let the bass of Heaven's deep organ blow;
And with your ninefold harmony
Make up full consort to the angelic symphony.

XIV

For if such holy song
Enwrap our fancy long,
    Time will run back and fetch the age of gold,
And speckled Vanity
Will sicken soon and die,
    And leprous Sin will melt from earthly mold,
And Hell itself will pass away,
And leave her dolorous mansions to the peering day.

XV

Yea, Truth and Justice then
Will down return to men,
    Orbed in a rainbow; and, like glories wearing,
Mercy will sit between,
Thorned in celestial sheen,
    With radiant feet the tissued clouds down steering;
And Heaven, as at some festival,
Will open wide the gates of her high palace hall.

XVI

But wisest Fate says no,
This must not yet be so;
    The Babe lies yet in smiling infancy,
That on the bitter cross

Must redeem our loss,
    So both himself and us to glorify;
Yet first to those ychained in sleep,
The wakeful trump of doom must thunder through the deep,

XVII

With such a horrid clang
As on Mount Sinai rang
    While the red fire and smoldering clouds outbrake:
The aged Earth aghast
With terror of that blast,
    Shall from the surface to the center shake,
When at the world's last session
The dreadful Judge in middle air shall spread his throne.

XVIII

And then at last our bliss
Full and perfect is,
    But now begins; for from this happy day
The old Dragon under ground,
In straiter limits bound,
    Not half so far casts his usurped sway,
And, wroth to see his kingdom fail,
Swinges the scaly horror of his folded tail.

XIX

The oracles are dumb,
No voice or hideous hum
    Runs through the arched roof in words deceiving.
Apollo from his shrine

Can no more divine,
    With hollow shriek the steep of Delphos leaving.
No nightly trance or breathed spell
Inspires the pale-eyed priest from the prophetic cell.

XX

The lonely mountains o'er,
And the resounding shore,
    A voice of weeping heard, and loud lament;
From haunted spring and dale,
Edged with poplar pale,
    The parting Genius is with sighing sent;
With flower-inwoven tresses torn
The nymphs in twilight shade of tangled thickets mourn.

XXI

In consecrated earth,
And on the holy hearth,
    The Lars and Lemures moan with midnight plaint;
In urns and altars round,
A drear and dying sound
    Affrights the flamens at their service quaint;
And the chill marble seems to sweat,
While each peculiar power forgoes his wonted seat.

XXII

Peor and Baalim
Forsake their temples dim,
    With that twice-battered god of Palestine;
And mooned Ashtaroth,

Heaven's queen and mother both,
    Now sits not girt with tapers' holy shine;
The Libyc Hammon shrinks his horn,
In vain the Tyrian maids their wounded Thammuz mourn.

XXIII

And sullen Moloch, fled,
Hath left in shadows dread
    His burning idol all of blackest hue;
In vain with cymbals' ring
They call the grisly king,
    In dismal dance about the furnace blue;
The brutish gods of Nile as fast,
Isis and Orus, and the dog Anubis, haste.

XXIV

Nor is Osiris seen
In Memphian grove or green,
    Trampling the unshowered grass with lowings loud;
Nor can he be at rest
Within his sacred chest,
    Nought but profoundest Hell can be his shroud;
In vain with timbreled anthems dark
The sable-stoled sorcerers bear his worshiped ark.

XXV

He feels from Juda's land
The dreaded Infant's hand,
    The rays of Bethlehem blind his dusky eyn;
Nor all the gods beside

Longer dare abide,
    Not Typhon huge ending in snaky twine:
Our Babe, to show his Godhead true,
Can in his swaddling bands control the damned crew.

XXVI

So when the sun in bed,
Curtained with cloudy red,
    Pillows his chin upon an orient wave,
The flocking shadows pale
Troop to the infernal jail;
    Each fettered ghost slips to his several grave,
And the yellow-skirted fays
Fly after the night-steeds, leaving their moon-loved maze.

XXVII

But see, the Virgin blest
Hath laid her Babe to rest.
    Time is our tedious song should here have ending;
Heaven's youngest-teemed star
Hath fixed her polished car,
    Her sleeping Lord with handmaid lamp attending;
And all about the courtly stable
Bright-harnessed angels sit in order serviceable.

The Birth of Christ

Alfred, Lord Tennyson

The time draws near the birth of Christ;
The moon is hid—the night is still;
The Christmas bells from hill to hill
Answer each other in the mist.

Four voices of four hamlets round,
From far and near, on mead and moor,
Swell out and fail, as if a door
Were shut between me and the sound.

Each voice four changes on the wind,
That now dilate and now decrease,
Peace and good-will, good-will and peace,
Peace and good-will to all mankind.

Rise, happy morn! rise, holy morn!
Draw forth the cheerful day from night;
O Father! touch the east, and light
The light that shone when hope was born!

The Three Kings

Henry Wadsworth Longfellow

Three Kings came riding from far away,
  Melchior and Gaspar and Baltasar;
Three Wise Men out of the East were they,
And they traveled by night and they slept by day,
  For their guide was a beautiful, wonderful star.

The star was so beautiful, large and clear,
  That all the other stars of the sky
Became a white mist in the atmosphere;
And by this they knew that the coming was near
  Of the Prince foretold in the prophecy.

Three caskets they bore on their saddle-bows,
  Three caskets of gold with golden keys;
Their robes were of crimson silk, with rows

Of bells and pomegranates and furbelows,
  Their turbans like blossoming almond-trees.

And so the Three Kings rode into the West,
  Through the dusk of night over hill and dell,
And sometimes they nodded with beard on breast,
And sometimes talked, as they paused to rest,
  With the people they met at some wayside well.

"Of the Child that is born," said Baltasar,
  "Good people, I pray you, tell us the news;
For we in the East have seen His star,
And have ridden fast, and have ridden far,
  To find and worship the King of the Jews."

And the people answered, "You ask in vain;
  We know of no king but Herod the Great!"
They thought the Wise Men were men insane,
As they spurred their horses across the plain
  Like riders in haste who cannot wait.

And when they came to Jerusalem,
  Herod the Great, who had heard this thing,
Sent for the Wise Men and questioned them;
And said, "Go down unto Bethlehem,
  And bring me tidings of this new king."

So they rode away, and the star stood still,
  The only one in the gray of morn;

Yes, it stopped, it stood still of its own free will,
Right over Bethlehem on the hill,
  The city of David where Christ was born.

And the Three Kings rode through the gate and the guard,
  Through the silent street, till their horses turned
And neighed as they entered the great inn-yard;
But the windows were closed, and the doors were barred,
  And only a light in the stable burned.

And cradled there in the scented hay,
  In the air made sweet by the breath of kine,
The little Child in the manger lay,
The Child that would be King one day
  Of a kingdom not human, but divine.

His mother, Mary of Nazareth,
  Sat watching beside his place of rest,
Watching the even flow of his breath,
For the joy of life and the terror of death
  Were mingled together in her breast.

They laid their offerings at his feet:
  The gold was their tribute to a King;
The frankincense, with its odor sweet,
Was for the Priest, the Paraclete;
  The myrrh for the body's burying.

And the mother wondered and bowed her head,
  And sat as still as a statue of stone;

Her heart was troubled yet comforted,
Remembering what the angel had said
   Of an endless reign and of David's throne.

Then the Kings rode out of the city gate,
   With a clatter of hoofs in proud array;
But they went not back to Herod the Great,
For they knew his malice and feared his hate,
   And returned to their homes by another way.

Christmas in the Olden Time

Sir Walter Scott

On Christmas-eve the bells were rung;
The damsel donned her kirtle sheen;
The hall was dressed with holly green;
Forth to the wood did merry men go,
To gather in the mistletoe.
Thus opened wide the baron's hall
To vassal, tenant, serf and all;
Power laid his rod of rule aside
And ceremony doffed his pride.
The heir, with roses in his shoes,
That night might village partner choose;
The lord, underogating, share
The vulgar game of "Post and Pair."
All hailed, with uncontrolled delight,
And general voice, the happy night

That to the cottage, as the crown,
Brought tidings of salvation down.

The fire, with well-dried logs supplied,
Went roaring up the chimney wide;
The huge hall-table's oaken face,
Scrubbed till it shone, the day to grace,
Bore then upon its massive board
No mark to part the squire and lord.
Then was brought in the lusty brawn
By old blue-coated serving man;
Then the grim boar's head frowned on high,
Crested with bays and rosemary.
Well can the green-garbed ranger tell
How, when and where the monster fell;
What dogs before his death he tore,
And all the baitings of the boar.
The wassal round, in good brown bowls,
Garnished with ribbons, blithely trowls.
There the huge sirloin reeked: hard by
Plum-porridge stood, and Christmas pye;
Nor failed old Scotland to produce,
At such high-tide, her savory goose.

Then came the merry maskers in,
And carols roared with blithesome din.
If unmelodious was the song,
It was a hearty note, and strong;
Who lists may in their murmuring see

Traces of ancient mystery;
White shirts supplied the masquerade,
And smutted cheeks the visors made;
But O, what maskers richly dight,
Can boast of bosoms half so light!
England was "merry England" when
Old Christmas brought his sports again;
'Twas Christmas broached the mightiest ale,
'Twas Christmas told the merriest tale;
A Christmas gambol oft would cheer
The poor man's heart through half the year.

Christmas at Sea

Robert Louis Stevenson

The sheets were frozen hard, and they cut the naked hand;
The decks were like a slide, where a seaman scarce could stand;
The wind was a nor'wester, blowing squally off the sea;
And cliffs and spouting breakers were the only things a-lee.
They heard the surf a-roaring before the break of day;
But 'twas only with the peep of light we saw how ill we lay.
We tumbled every hand on deck instanter, with a shout,
And we gave her the maintops'l, and stood by to go about.

All day we tacked and tacked between the South Head and the
North;
All day we hauled the frozen sheets, and got no further forth;
All day as cold as charity, in bitter pain and dread,
For very life and and nature we tacked from head to head.

We gave the South a wider berth, for there the tide race roared;
But every tack we made we brought the North Head close aboard:
So's we saw the cliffs and houses, and the breakers running high,
And the coastguard in his garden, with his glass against his eye.

The frost was on the village roofs as white as ocean foam;
The good red fires were burning bright in every 'longshore home;
The windows sparkled clear, and the chimneys volleyed out;
And I vow we sniffed the victuals as the vessel went about.

The bells upon the church were rung with a mighty jovial cheer;
For it's just that I should tell you how (of all days in the year)
This day of our adversity was blessèd Christmas morn.
And the house above the coastguard's was the house where I was
born.

O well I saw the pleasant room, the pleasant faces there,
My mother's silver spectacles, my father's silver hair;
And well I saw the firelight, like a flight of homely elves,
Go dancing round the china-plates that stand upon the shelves.

And well I knew the talk they had, the talk that was of me,
Of the shadow on the household and the son that went to sea;
And O the wicked fool I seemed, in every kind of way,
To be here and hauling frozen ropes on blessèd Christmas Day.

They lit the high sea-light, and the dark began to fall.
"All hands to loose topgallant sails," I heard the captain call.
"By the Lord, she'll never stand it," our first mate, Jackson, cried.
. . . "It's the one way or the other, Mr. Jackson," he replied.

She staggered to her bearings, but the sails were new and good,
And the ship smelt up to windward just as though she understood.
As the winter's day was ending, in the entry of the night,
We cleared the weary headland, and passed below the light.

And they heaved a mighty breath, every soul on board but me,
As they saw her nose again pointing handsome out to sea;
But all that I could think of, in the darkness and the cold,
Was just that I was leaving home and my folks were growing old.

A Christmas Greeting

(FROM A NORTHERN STAR-GROUP TO A SOUTHERN. 1889–90)

Walt Whitman

Welcome, Brazilian brother—thy ample place is ready;
A loving hand—a smile from the north—a sunny instant hail!
(Let the future care for itself, where it reveals its troubles,
impedimentas,
Ours, ours the present throe, the democratic aim, the acceptance
and the faith;)
To thee to-day our reaching arm, our turning neck—to thee from
us the expectant eye,
Thou cluster free! thou brilliant lustrous one! thou, learning well,
The true lesson of a nation's light in the sky,
(More shining than the Cross, more than the Crown,)
The height to be superb humanity.

A Visit from St. Nicholas

Clement Clarke Moore

'Twas the night before Christmas, when all through the house
Not a creature was stirring, not even a mouse;
The stockings were hung by the chimney with care,
In hopes that St. Nicholas soon would be there.
The children were nestled all snug in their beds,
While visions of sugar-plums danced through their heads;
And mamma in her kerchief, and I in my cap,
Had just settled our brains for a long winter's nap—
When out on the lawn there arose such a clatter,
I sprang from my bed to see what was the matter.
Away to the window I flew like a flash,
Tore open the shutters and threw up the sash.
The moon on the breast of the new-fallen snow
Gave the lustre of midday to objects below;
When, what to my wondering eyes should appear,
But a miniature sleigh and eight tiny reindeer,

With a little old driver, so lively and quick,
I knew in a moment it must be St. Nick.
More rapid than eagles his coursers they came,
And he whistled, and shouted, and called them by name:
"Now, Dasher! now, Dancer! now, Prancer! and Vixen!
On, Comet! on, Cupid! on, Donder and Blitzen!
To the top of the porch! to the top of the wall!
Now dash away! dash away! dash away all!"
As dry leaves that before the wild hurricane fly,
When they meet with an obstacle, mount to the sky,
So up to the house-top the coursers they flew,
With the sleighful of toys, and St. Nicholas too.
And then in a twinkling I heard on the roof
The prancing and pawing of each little hoof.
As I drew in my head, and was turning around,
Down the chimney St. Nicholas came with a bound.
He was dressed all in fur from his head to his foot,
And his clothes were all tarnished with ashes and soot;
A bundle of toys he had flung on his back,
And he looked like a peddlar just opening his pack.
His eyes, how they twinkled! his dimples, how merry!
His cheeks were like roses, his nose like a cherry!
His droll little mouth was drawn up like a bow,
And the beard on his chin was as white as the snow.
The stump of a pipe he held tight in his teeth,
And the smoke, it encircled his head like a wreath.
He had a broad face, and a little round belly
That shook, when he laughed, like a bowl full of jelly.
He was chubby and plump—a right jolly old elf;
And I laughed, when I saw him, in spite of myself.

A wink of his eye, and a twist of his head
Soon gave me to know I had nothing to dread.
He spoke not a word, but went straight to his work,
And filled all the stockings; then turned with a jerk,
And laying his finger aside of his nose,
And giving a nod, up the chimney he rose.
He sprang to his sleigh, to the team gave a whistle,
And away they all flew, like the down of a thistle,
But I heard him exclaim, ere he drove out of sight,
"Happy Christmas to all, and to all a good-night!"

Songs and Carols

Some of the lines of these songs,
a few of them dating back many hundreds of years,
are among the best remembered relics of childhood,
learned in a time we barely remember,
yet never forgotten.

God Rest You Merry, Gentlemen

Traditional

God rest you merry, gentlemen,
  Let nothing you dismay,
For Jesus Christ, our Saviour,
  Was born upon this day.
To save us all from Satan's pow'r
  When we were gone astray.
    O tidings of comfort and joy!
    For Jesus Christ, our Saviour,
    Was born on Christmas Day.

In Bethlehem, in Jewry,
  This blessed Babe was born,
And laid within a manger,
  Upon this blessed morn;
The which His mother, Mary,
  Nothing did take in scorn.

From God our Heavenly Father,
  A blessed angel came;
And unto certain shepherds
  Brought tidings of the same:
How that in Bethlehem was born
  The Son of God by name.

"Fear not," then said the angel,
  "Let nothing you affright,
This day is born a Saviour
  Of virtue, power, and might,
So frequently to vanquish all
  The friends of Satan quite."

The shepherds at those tidings
  Rejoicèd much in mind,
And left their flocks a-feeding
  In tempest, storm, and wind,
And went to Bethlehem straightway,
  This blessed Babe to find.

But when to Bethlehem they came,
  Whereat this infant lay,
They found Him in a manger,
  Where oxen feed on hay,
His mother Mary kneeling,
  Unto the Lord did pray.

Now to the Lord sing praises,
  All you within this place,

And with true love and brotherhood
  Each other now embrace;
This holy tide of Christmas
  All others doth deface.
    O tidings of comfort and joy!
  For Jesus Christ, our Saviour,
    Was born on Christmas Day.

We Three Kings of Orient Are

John Henry Hopkins

All: We three kings of Orient are,
Bearing gifts we traverse afar,
Field and fountain, moor and mountain,
Following yonder star.

O star of wonder, star of night,
Star with royal beauty bright,
Westward leading, still proceeding,
Guide us to thy perfect light.

Melchior: Born a king on Bethlehem's plain,
Gold I bring, to crown Him again,
King for ever, ceasing never,
Over us all to reign.

Caspar: Frankincense to offer have I,
Incense owns a Deity nigh,
Prayer and praising, all men raising,
Worship Him, God most high.

Balthazar: Myrrh is mine, its bitter perfume
Breathes a life of gathering gloom;
Sorrowing, sighing, bleeding, dying,
Sealed in the stone-cold tomb.

All: Glorious now behold Him arise,
King and God and sacrifice,
Alleluia, alleluia;
Earth to the heavens replies.

THE TWELVE DAYS OF CHRISTMAS (A PARTRIDGE IN A PEAR TREE)

Traditional

On the first day of Christmas my true love sent to me
A partridge in a pear tree.
On the second day of Christmas my true love sent to me
Two turtle doves and a partridge in a pear tree.
On the third day of Christmas my true love sent to me
Three French hens, two turtle doves, and a partridge in a pear tree.
On the fourth day of Christmas my true love sent to me
Four colly birds, three French hens, two turtle doves, and a partridge in a pear tree.
On the fifth day of Christmas my true love sent to me
Five gold rings, four colly birds, three French hens, two turtle doves, and a partridge in a pear tree.
On the sixth day of Christmas my true love sent to me
Six geese a-laying, five gold rings, four colly birds, three French hens, two turtle doves, and a partridge in a pear tree.

On the seventh day of Christmas my true love sent to me
Seven swans a-swimming, six geese a-laying, five gold rings, four colly birds, three French hens, two turtle doves, and a partridge in a pear tree.
On the eighth day of Christmas my true love sent to me
Eight maids a-milking, seven swans a-swimming, six geese a-laying, five gold rings, four colly birds, three French hens, two turtle doves, and a partridge in a pear tree.
On the ninth day of Christmas my true love sent to me
Nine ladies dancing, eight maids a-milking, seven swans a-swimming, six geese a-laying, five gold rings, four colly birds, three French hens, two turtle doves, and a partridge in a pear tree.
On the tenth day of Christmas my true love sent to me
Ten lords a-leaping, nine ladies dancing, eight maids a-milking, seven swans a-swimming, six geese a-laying, five gold rings, four colly birds, three French hens, two turtle doves, and a partridge in a pear tree.
On the eleventh day of Christmas my true love sent to me
Eleven drummers drumming, ten lords a-leaping, nine ladies dancing, eight maids a-milking, seven swans a-swimming, six geese a-laying, five gold rings, four colly birds, three French hens, two turtle doves, and a partridge in a pear tree.
On the twelfth day of Christmas my true love sent to me
Twelve pipers piping, eleven drummers drumming, ten lords a-leaping, nine ladies dancing, eight maids a-milking, seven swans a-swimming, six geese a-laying, five gold rings, four colly birds, three French hens, two turtle doves, and a partridge in a pear tree.

Good King Wenceslas

J. M. Neale (1818–1866)

Good King Wenceslas look'd out
   On the feast of Stephen,
When the snow lay round about,
   Deep and crisp and even.
Brightly shone the moon that night,
   Though the frost was cruel,
When a poor man came in sight,
   Gathering winter fuel.

"Hither, page, and stand by me,
   If thou know'st it, telling,
Yonder peasant, who is he?
   Where and what his dwelling?"
"Sire, he lives a good league hence,
   Underneath the mountain;

Right against the forest fence,
By Saint Agnes' fountain."

"Bring me flesh and bring me wine,
Bring me pine-logs hither;
Thou and I will see him dine,
When we bear them thither."
Page and monarch, forth they went,
Forth they went together;
Through the rude wind's wild lament,
And the bitter weather.

"Sire, the night is darker now,
And the wind blows stronger;
Fails my heart, I know not how,
I can go no longer."
"Mark my footsteps, good my page,
Tread thou in them boldly;
Thou shalt find the winter's rage
Freeze thy blood less coldly."

In his master's steps he trod,
Where the snow lay dinted;
Heat was in the very sod
Which the saint had printed.
Therefore, Christian men, be sure,
Wealth or rank possessing,
Ye who now will bless the poor,
Shall yourselves find blessing.

I Saw Three Ships

Fifteenth Century

I saw three ships come sailing in
   On Christmas day, on Christmas day;
I saw three ships some sailing in
   On Christmas day in the morning.

And what was in those ships all three
   On Christmas day, on Christmas day . . .

Our Saviour Christ and His lady,
   On Christmas day, on Christmas day . . .

Pray whither sailed those ships all three
   On Christmas day, on Christmas day . . .

O they sailed into Bethlehem
   On Christmas day, on Christmas day . . .

And all the bells on earth shall ring
  On Christmas day, on Christmas day . . .

And all the angels in heaven shall sing
  On Christmas day, on Christmas day . . .

And all the souls on earth shall sing
  On Christmas day, on Christmas day . . .

Then let us all rejoice amain!
  On Christmas day, on Christmas day . . .

Jingle Bells

J. Pierpont (1857)

Dashing thro' the snow,
In a one-horse open sleigh;
O'er the fields we go,
Laughing all the way;
Bells on bob-tail ring
Making spirits bright;
What fun it is to ride and sing
A sleighing song to-night!

Chorus: Accompanied by jingling glasses.

Jingle, bells! Jingle, bells!
Jingle all the way!
Oh! what fun it is to ride
In a one-horse open sleigh!
Jingle, bells! Jingle, bells!

Jingle all the way!
Oh! what fun it is to ride
In a one-horse open sleigh!

A day or two ago
I thought I'd take a ride,
And soon Miss Fannie Bright
Was seated by my side.
The horse was lean and lank;
Misfortune seem'd his lot;
He got into a drifted bank,
And we, we got up-sot.

Now the ground is white;
Go it while you're young;
Take the girls to-night,
And sing this sleighing song.
Just get a bob-tail'd bay,
Two-forty for his speed;
Then hitch him to an open sleigh,
And crack! you'll take the lead.

The Holly and the Ivy

Fifteenth Century

The Holly and the Ivy,
  When they are both full grown
Of all the trees are in the wood,
  The Holly bears the crown.

O the rising of the sun,
  And the running of the deer,
The playing of the merry organ,
  Sweet singing in the choir.

The Holly bears a blossom
  As white as any flower;
And Mary bore sweet Jesus Christ
  To be our sweet Saviour.

The Holly bears a berry
  As red as any blood;
And Mary bore sweet Jesus Christ
  To do poor sinners good.

The Holly bears a prickle
  As sharp as any thorn;
And Mary bore sweet Jesus Christ
  On Christmas in the morn.

The Holly bears a bark
  As bitter as any gall;
And Mary bore sweet Jesus Christ
  For to redeem us all.

The Holly and the Ivy
  Now both are full well grown:
Of all the trees are in the wood
  The Holly bears the crown.

O Come, All Ye Faithful

Latin, Eighteenth Century

O come, all ye faithful,
Joyful and triumphant;
O come ye, O come ye to Bethlehem;
Come and behold Him
Born the King of angels;

O come, let us adore Him,
O come, let us adore Him,
O come, let us adore Him,
Christ the Lord.

Sing, choirs of angels,
Sing in exultation,
Sing all ye citizens of heav'n above:
Glory to God
In the highest.

O come, let us adore Him,
O come, let us adore Him,
O come, let us adore Him,
Christ the Lord.

Yea Lord, we greet Thee,
Born this happy morning;
Jesus to Thee be glory giv'n;
Word of the Father,
Now in flesh appearing.

O come, let us adore Him,
O come, let us adore Him,
O come, let us adore Him,
Christ the Lord.

Angels We Have Heard on High

Traditional French

Angels we have heard on high,
sweetly singing o'er the plains;
And the mountains in reply
Echoing their joyous strains

Gloria in excelsis Deo,
Gloria in excelsis Deo.

Shepherds, why this jubilee?
Why your joyous songs prolong?
What the gladsome tidings be
Which inspire your heav'nly song?

Gloria in excelsis Deo,
Gloria in excelsis Deo.

Come to Bethlehem, and see
Him whose birth the angels sing;
Come, adore on bended knee,
Christ, the Lord, our new-born King.

Gloria in excelsis Deo,
Gloria in excelsis Deo.

What Child Is This? (Greensleeves)

Old English

What Child is this, who, laid to rest,
On Mary's lap is sleeping?
Whom angels greet with anthems sweet,
While shepherds watch are keeping?
This, this is Christ, the King,
Whom shepherds guard and angels sing:
Haste, haste to bring him laud,
The Babe, the Son of Mary!

So bring Him incense, gold and myrrh,
Come peasant, king to own Him;
The King of Kings, salvation brings:
Let loving hearts enthrone Him.
Raise, raise the song on high,
The Virgin sings her lullaby:
Joy, joy for Christ is born,
The Babe, the son of Mary!

The First Noel

Traditional

The first Noel the angel did say,
Was to certain poor shepherds in fields as they lay;
In fields where they lay keeping their sheep
On a cold winter's night that was so deep.

Noel, Noel, Noel, Noel,
Born is the King of Israel.

They looked up and saw a star
Shining in the East, beyond them far.
And to the earth it gave great light,
And so it continued both day and night.

Noel, Noel, Noel, Noel,
Born is the King of Israel.

This star drew them to the northwest,
O'er Bethlehem it took its rest.
And there it did both stop and stay,
Right over the place where Jesus lay.

Noel, Noel, Noel, Noel,
Born is the King of Israel.

Then entered in those wise men three,
Fell reverently upon their knee,
And offered there in His presence,
Their gold, and myrrh, and frankincense.

Noel, Noel, Noel, Noel,
Born is the King of Israel.

Then let us all with one accord
Sing praises to our heavenly Lord;
That hath made heaven and earth of naught,
And with His blood mankind has brought.

Noel, Noel, Noel, Noel,
Born is the King of Israel.

O Little Town of Bethlehem

Phillips Brooks (1835–1893)

O little town of Bethlehem!
How still we see thee lie;
Above thy deep and dreamless sleep
The silent stars go by;
Yet in thy dark streets shineth
The everlasting Light;
The hopes and fears of all the years
Are met in thee tonight.

For Christ is born of Mary,
And gathered all above,
While mortals sleep, the angels keep
Their watch of wondering love.
O morning stars, together
Proclaim the holy birth!

And praises sing to God the King,
And peace to men on earth.

How silently, how silently,
The wondrous gift is giv'n!
So God imparts to human hearts
The blessings of His heav'n.
No ear may hear His coming,
But in this world of sin,
Where meek souls will receive Him still,
The dear Christ enters in.

O holy Child of Bethlehem!
Descend to us, we pray;
Cast out our sin and enter in,
Be born in us today.
We hear the Christmas angels
The great glad tidings tell;
O come to us, abide with us,
Our Lord Emmanuel!

Away in a Manger

German Children's Carol

Away in a manger, no crib for His bed,
The little Lord Jesus laid down His sweet head.
The stars in the sky, looked down where He lay,
The little Lord Jesus asleep in the hay.

The cattle are lowing, the poor baby wakes,
But little Lord Jesus, no crying He makes.
I love Thee, Lord Jesus, look down from the sky,
And stay by my cradle till morning is nigh.

Coventry Carol (Lullaby, Thou Little Tiny Child)

Robert Croo (d. 1534)

Lullaby, Thou little tiny Child,
By, by, lully, lullay:
Lullay, Thou little tiny child,
By, by, lully, lullay.

O sisters too, how may we do
For to preserve this day,
This poor Youngling for whom we sing,
By, by, lully, lullay?

Herod the king in his raging,
Charged he hath this day,
His men of might, in his own sight,
All children young to slay.

Then woe is me, poor Child, for Thee,
And ever mourn and say,
For Thy parting nor say, nor sing,
By, by, lully, lullay.

O, How Joyfully
(O Sanctissima)

Sicilian Hymn

O how joyfully, O how merrily
Christmas comes with its grace divine!
Grace again is beaming, Christ the world redeeming;
Hail, ye Christians, Hail the joyous Christmas time!

O how joyfully, O how merrily
Christmas comes with its peace divine!
Peace on earth is reigning, Christ our peace regaining;
Hail, ye Christians, Hail the joyous Christmas time!

O how joyfully, O how merrily
Christmas comes with its life divine!
Angels high in glory, Chant the Christmas story;
Hail, ye Christians, Hail the joyous Christmas time!

SAMUEL PEPYS'S TWELVE DAYS OF CHRISTMAS

Samuel Pepys (1633–1703) kept one of the best known of all diaries. Between January 1, 1660 and May 31, 1669, he recorded for himself minute details of his life in London. Helped by the patronage of a cousin Sir Edward Montagu, Earl of Sandwich (the "My Lord" of the diary), Pepys had secured a post as a clerk in the Navy office and was later Secretary to the Admiralty, a position that brought him into frequent contact with the court and King Charles II. He lived through a tumultuous time—the Restoration, the Great Plague of London of 1665, and the Great Fire the following year, all the while writing his observations in a private cipher. After his death, his diary was deposited at Magdalene College, Cambridge, and was only published in 1825 after an undergraduate spent three years deciphering Pepys's code. Following are a few selections of entries from Pepys's Twelve Days of Christmas.

1660

December 27th

About the middle of the night I was very ill—I think with eating and drinking too much—and so I was forced to call the maid, who pleased my wife and I in her running up and down so innocently in her smock, and vomited in the basin, and so to sleep, and in the morning was pretty well, only got cold, and so had pain . . . as I used to have.

December 31st

At the office all morning, and after that home; and not staying to dine I went out, and in Paul's Churchyard I bought the play of "Henry the Fourth," and so went to the new Theatre and saw it acted; but my expectation being too great, it did not please me as otherwise I believe it would; and my having a book I believe did spoil it a little.

1661

December 30th

At the office, and so with my wife and Sir W. Pen to see our pictures, which do not much displease us, and so back again; and I staid at the Mitre, whither I had invited my old acquaintance of the Exchequer to a good chine of beef, which with three barrels of oysters and three pullets, and plenty of wine and mirth, was our dinner, and there was about twelve of us. I made them a foolish promise to give them one this day twelvemonth, and so for ever while I live; but I do not intend it.

December 31st

After supper, and my barber had trimmed me, I sat down to end my journell for this year, and my condition at this time, by God's blessing is thus: my health is very good, and so is my wife's in all respects. . . . I suppose myself to be worth about £500 clear in the world. . . . But my greatest trouble is that I have for this last half year been a very great spendthrift in all manner of respects, that I am afeard to cast up my accounts, though I hope I am worth what I say above. . . . I have newly taken a solemn oath about abstaining from plays and wine, which I am resolved to keep according to the letter of the oath which I keep by me.

1662

January 1st

Waking this morning out of my sleep on a sudden, I did with my elbow hit my wife a great blow over her face and nose, which waked her with pain, at which I was sorry, and to sleep again.

December 25th

Up pretty early, leaving my wife not well in bed, and with my boy walked, it being a most brave cold and dry frosty morning, and had a pleasant walk to White Hall, where I intended to have received the Communion with the family, but I came a little too late. . . .

Dined by my wife's bed-side with great content, having a mess of brave plum-porridge and a roasted pullet for dinner, and I sent for a mince-pie abroad, my wife not being well to make any herself yet.

December 26th

Up, my wife to the making of Christmas pies all day, being now pretty well again, and I abroad to the Wardrobe.

December 30th

After dinner drinking five or six glasses of wine, which liberty I now take till I begin my oath again, I went home and took my wife into coach, and carried her to Westminster; thence to White Hall, where I carried my wife to see the Queen in her presence-chamber; and the maydes of honour and the young Duke of Monmouth playing at cards. Some of them, and but a few, were very pretty; though all well dressed in velvet gowns.

December 31st

Thence merry back, Mr. Povy and I, to White Hall; he carrying me thither on purpose to carry me into the ball this night before the King. All the way he talking very ingeniously, and I find him a fine gentleman, and one that loves to live nobly and neatly, as I perceive by his discourse of his house, pictures, and horses. He brought me first to the Duke's chamber, where I saw him and the Duchess at supper; and thence into the room where the ball was to be, crammed with fine ladies, the greatest of the Court. By and by comes the King and Queen, the Duke [later King James II] and Duchess, and all the great ones: and after seating themselves, the King takes out the Duchess of York; and the Duke, the Duchess of Buckingham; the Duke of Monmouth, my Lady Castlemaine; and so other lords other ladies: and they danced the Bransle. After that, the King led a lady a single Coranto; and then the rest of the lords, one after another, other ladies: very noble it was, and great pleasure to see. . . .

Thus ends this year with great mirth to me and my wife. . . . In fine, for the good condition of myself, wife, family, and estate, in the great degree that it is, and for the public state of the nation, so quiett as it is, the Lord God be praised!

1663

January 6th

Up and Mr. Creed brought a pot of chocolate ready made for our morning draft, and then he and I to the Duke's. . . . This night making an end wholly of Christmas, with a mind fully satisfied with the great pleasures we have had by being abroad from home; and I do find my mind so apt to run to its old want of pleasures, that it is high time to betake myself to my late vows, which I will tomorrow, God willing, perfect and bind myself to; that so I may for a great while, do my duty, as I have well begun, and increase my good name and esteem in the world, and get money, which sweetens all things, and whereof I have much need.

Saw "Twelfth Night" acted well, though it be but a silly play, and not related at all to the name or day.

December 25th

Lay long talking pleasantly with my wife, but among other things she begun, I know not whether by design or chance, to enquire what she should do if I should by any accident die, to which I did give her some slight answer; but shall make good use of it to bring myself to some settlement for her sake, by making a will as soon as I can.

December 27th

Up and to church alone, and so home to dinner with my wife, very pleasant and pleased with one another's company, and in our general enjoyment of one another better we think than most other couples do. So after dinner to the French church, but came too late, and so back to our owne church, where I slept all the sermon, the Scott preaching, and so home.

December 31st

Sat till 4 o'clock in the morning making up my accounts and writing this last Journall of the year. And first I bless God I do find that I am worth in money above £800. . . .

1664

January 1st

My wife and I went to the Duke's house, the first play I have been at these six months, according to my last vowe, and here saw the much cried-up play of "Henry the Eighth"; which, though I went with resolution to like it, is so simple a thing made up of a great many patches, that besides the shows and processions in it there is nothing in the world good or well done.

January 2nd

After dinner I took my wife out, for I do find that I am not able to conquer myself as to going to plays till I come to a new vowe concerning it, and that I am now come, that is to say, that I will not see above one in a month at any of the publique theatres till the sum of 50*s.* be spent, and then none before New Year's Day next, unless that I do become worth £1,000 sooner than then, and then am free to come to some other terms. . . .

So to the King's house, and saw "The Usurper," which is no good play, though better than what I saw yesterday. However we rose unsatisfied, and took coach and home.

January 4th

To the Tennis Court and there saw the King play at Tennis, and others: but to see how the King's play was extolled without any cause at all was a loathsome sight, though sometimes indeed he did play very well and deserved to be commended; but such open flattery is beastly.

December 31st

At the office all the morning, and after dinner there again, dispatched first my letters, and then to my accounts, not of the month but of the whole yeare also, and was at it till past twelve at night, it being bitter cold; but yet I was well satisfied with my worke. . . . Thence home to eat a little and to bed. Soon as ever the clock struck one, I kissed my wife in the kitchen by the fireside, wishing her a merry new yeare, observing that I believe I was the first proper wisher of it this year, for I did it as soon as ever the clock struck one. . . .

I bless God I never have been in so good plight as to my health. . . . But I am at a great losse to know whether it be my hare's foote, or taking every morning of a pill of turpentine, or my having left off the wearing of a gowne. This Christmas I judged it fit to look over all my papers and books; and to tear all that I found either boyish or not to be worth keeping, or fit to be seen, if it should please God to take me away suddenly.

1665

December 25th

To church in the morning and there saw a wedding in the church, which I have not seen many a day; and the young people so merry one with another. And strange to see what delight we married people have to see these poor fools decoyed into our condition, every man and woman gazing and smiling at them.

December 30th

Up and to the office; at noon home to dinner, and all the afternoon to my accounts, and there find myself to my great joy a great deal worth above £4,000, for which the Lord be praised!

1666

December 25th

Lay pretty long in bed, and then rose, leaving my wife desirous to sleep, having sat up till four this morning seeing her mayds make mince-pies. I to church, where our parson Mills made a good sermon. Then home, and dined well on some good ribbs of beef roasted and mince-pies; only my wife, brother, and Barker; and plenty of good wine of my owne, and my heart full of true joy and thanks to God Almighty for the goodness of my condition at this day. After dinner I begun to teach my wife and Barker my song, "It is decreed," which pleases me mightily as now I have Mr. Hinxton's base.

December 27th

Up; and called up by the King's trumpets, which cost me 10*s.* So to the office, where we sat all the morning. From hence to the Duke's house, and there saw "Macbeth" most excellently acted, and a most excellent play for variety.

December 31st

Rising this day with a full design to mind nothing else but to make up my accounts for the year past, I did take money and walk forth to several places in the towne as far as the New Exchange to pay all my debts, it being still a very great frost and good walking.

1667

January 1st

Lay long, being a bitter, cold, frosty day, the frost being now grown old, and the Thames covered with ice. Up, and to the office, where all the morning busy.

January 4th

Up and seeing things put in order for a dinner at my house to-day. . . . Anon comes our company. . . . I did make them all gaze to see themselves served so nobly in plate, and a neat dinner, indeed, though but of seven dishes. Mighty merry I was and made them all, and they mightily pleased. . . . To cards, and then to sing and talk, and at night to sup, and then to cards; and last of all to have a flaggon of ale and apples, drunk out of a wood cupp as a Christmas draught, made all merry; and they full of admiration at my plate, particularly my flaggons (which indeed are noble). And so late home, all with great mirth and satisfaction to them, as I thought, and to myself to see all I have and do so much outdo for neatness and plenty anything done by any of them.

December 25th

It being a fine, light, moonshine morning, and so home round the city, and stopped and dropped money at five or six places, which I was the willinger to do, it being Christmas-day, and so home, and there find my wife in bed, and Jane and the maids making pyes, and so I to bed, and slept well, and rose about nine, and to church.

December 28th

Up, and to the office, where busy all the morning. . . . With my wife and girle to the King's house, and there saw "The Mad Couple," which is but an ordinary play; but only Nell's and Hart's mad parts are most excellently done, but especially her's: which makes it a miracle to me to think how ill she do any serious part, as the other day, just like a fool or changeling, and in a mad part do beyond all imitation almost.

1668

January 1st

Thence I after dinner to the Duke of York's playhouse, and there saw "Sir Martin Mar-all"; which I have seen so often, and yet am mightily pleased with it, and think it mighty witty, and the fullest of proper matter for mirth that ever was writ; and I do clearly see that they do improve in their acting of it. Here a mighty company of citizens, 'prentices, and others; and it makes me observe, that when I begun first to be able to bestow a play on myself, I do not remember that I saw so many by half of the ordinary 'prentices and mean people in the pit at 2*s.* 6*d.* a-piece as now; I going for several years no higher than the 12*d.* And then the 18*d.* places, though I strained hard to go in then when I did: so much the vanity and prodigality of the age is to be observed in this particular.

January 2nd

Up, and with Sir J. Minnes by coach to White Hall, and there attended the King and the Duke of York in the Duke of York's lodgings, with the rest of the Officers and many of the Commanders of the fleete, and some of our master shipwrights. Mr. Wren whispered me in the eare, and said that the Duke of Albemarle had put it into his Narrative for the House, that not above twenty-five ships fought in the engagement wherein he was, and that another was brought into his ship that had been turned out of his place when he was a boatswain, not long before, for being a drunkard. And the Prince said to me, standing by me, "God damn me, if they will turn out every man that will be drunk, they must turn out all the commanders in the fleete. What is the matter if he be drunk, so when he comes to fight he do his work? At least, let him be punished for his drunkenness, and not put out of his command presently." This he spoke, very much concerned for this idle fellow, one Greene.

January 6th

Up, leaving my wife to get her ready, and the maids to get a supper ready against night for our company; and I by coach to White Hall. Home, where we find my house with good fires and candles ready, and our Office the like, and the two Mercers, and Betty Turner, Pendleton, and W. Batelier. And so with much pleasure we into the house, and there fell to dancing, having extraordinary musick, two viollins, and a base viollin, and theorbo, four hands, the Duke of Buckingham's musique, the best in towne, sent me by Greeting, and there we set in to dancing. By and by to my house, to a very good supper, and mighty merry, and good musick playing; and after supper to dancing and singing till about twelve at night; and then we had a good sack posset for them, and an excellent cake, cost me near 20*s.*, of our Jane's making, which was cut into twenty pieces, there being by this time so many of our company, by the coming in of young Goodyer and some others of our neighbours, young men that could dance, hearing of our dancing; and anon comes in Mrs. Turner, the mother, and brings with her Mrs. Hollworthy, which pleased me mightily. And so to dancing again, and singing, with extraordinary great pleasure, till about two in the morning, and then broke up. I paid the fiddlers £3 among the four, and so away to bed, wearing and mightily pleased, and have the happiness to reflect upon it as I do sometimes on other things, as going to a play or the like, to be the greatest real comfort that I am to expect in the world, and that it is that that we do really labour in the hopes of; and so I do really enjoy myself, and understand that if I do not do it now I shall not hereafter, it may be, be able to pay for it, or have health to take pleasure in it, and so fill myself with vain expectation of pleasure and go without it.

December 25th

Up, and continued on my waistcoat, the first day this winter and I to church. . . . So home, and to dinner alone with my wife, who, poor wretch! sat undressed all day, till ten at night, altering and lacing of a noble petticoat: while I by her, making the boy read to me the Life of Julius Caesar, and Des Cartes' book of Musick, the latter of which I understand not, nor think he did well that writ it, though a most learned man. Then after supper I made the boy play upon his lute, . . . and so, my mind in mighty content, we to bed.

December 26th

Lay long with pleasure, prating with my wife, and then up, and a little to the Office.

December 28th

Up, called up by drums and trumpets; these things and boxes having cost me much money this Christmas already, and will do more.

1669

January 1st

Up, and presented from Captain Beckford with a noble silver warming-pan, which I am doubtful whether to take or no.

January 4th

Lay long talking with my wife, and did of my own accord come to an allowance of her of £30 a-year for all expenses, clothes and everything, which she was mightily pleased with, it being more than she ever asked or expected.

Recipes from Mrs. Beeton's One Shilling Cookery Book

The works of Mrs. Isabella Beeton (1836–1865) could be found in almost every Victorian kitchen. Her most famous book was Mrs Beeton's Book of Houshold Management *(1861), 1,350 pages of recipes and directions for managing the home, the staff, and the children.*

The following recipes come from a cheap shilling (about 8¢) edition of her cooking tips (how to furnish the kitchen of a small house for under £8) and recipes published around the time of Queen Victoria's Jubilee in 1897. Note that the costs are given in pre-decimalization terms: pounds (£); shillings (s.) and pence (d.). There were twelve pence to a shilling and twenty shillings to a pound.

ROAST GOOSE

INGREDIENTS

goose
- 4 large onions
- 10 sage-leaves
- ¼ lb. bread crumbs
- 1½ oz. butter

salt and pepper to taste
- 1 egg

CHOOSING AND TRUSSING

Select a goose with a clean white skin, plump breast, and yellow feet: if these latter are red, the bird is old. Should the weather permit, let it hang for a few days. Pluck, singe, draw, and carefully wash and wipe the goose; cut off the neck close to the back, leaving the skin long enough to turn over; cut off the feet at the first joint, and separate the pinions at the first joint. Beat the breast-bone flat with a rolling-pin, put a skewer through the under part of each wing, and, having drawn up the legs closely, put a skewer into the middle of each, and pass the same quite through the body. Insert another skewer into the small of the leg, bring it close down to the side-bone, run it through, and do the same to the other side. Cut off the end of the vent, and make a hole in the skin sufficiently large for the passage of the rump, in order to keep in the seasoning.

MODE

Make a sage-and-onion stuffing of the above ingredients by recipe for stuffing (see page 202); put it into the body of the goose, and secure it firmly at both ends, by passing the rump through the hole made in the skin, and the other end by tying the skin of the neck to the back. Put it down to a brisk fire, keep it well basted, and roast from 1½ to 2 hours. Remove the skewers, and serve with a tureen of good gravy, and one of apple sauce. Should a very highly-flavoured seasoning be preferred, the onions should not be parboiled, but minced raw. A ragoût, or pie, should be made of the giblets, or they may be stewed down to make gravy. Only a small quantity of gravy should be poured round the goose, and the remainder sent in a tureen.

TIME: A large goose, 1¾ hour; a moderate-sized one, 1¼ to 1½ hour.

Average cost: from 8*s.* upwards each.

Sufficient for 8 or nine persons.

Seasonable from September to March; but in perfection from Michaelmas to Christmas.

NOTE: A teaspoonful of made mustard, a saltspoonful of salt, a few grains of cayenne, mixed with a glass of port wine, are sometimes poured into the goose by a slit made in the apron.

SAGE-AND-ONION STUFFING FOR GEESE, DUCKS, AND PORK

INGREDIENTS

- 4 large onions
- 10 sage-leaves
- ¼ lb. bread crumbs
- 1½ oz. butter
- salt and pepper
- 1 egg

MODE

Peel the onions, put them into boiling water, simmer for 5 minutes, or rather longer, and put in the sage leaves for a minute or two to take off their rawness. Chop both very fine, add the bread, seasoning, and butter, and work the whole together with the yolk of an egg, when the stuffing will be ready for use. It should be rather highly seasoned, and the sage leaves finely chopped. Many cooks do not parboil the onions, but use them raw. The stuffing then is not so mild. When made for goose, a portion of the liver of the bird, simmered for a few minutes and very finely minced, is frequently added. The egg may be dispensed with.

TIME: Rather more than 5 minutes to simmer the onions.

Average cost, for this quantity: 5*d.*

Sufficient for 1 goose, or a pair of ducks.

MINCE PIES

INGREDIENTS

Good puff-paste (see pages 204 and 205)
Mincemeat (see page 206)

MODE

Make some good puff-paste by either of the above recipes; roll it out to the thickness of about ¼ inch, and line some good-sized patty-pans with it; fill them with mincemeat, cover with the paste, and cut it off all round close to the edge of the tin; put the pies into a brisk oven to draw the paste up, and bake for 25 minutes, or longer; brush them over with the white of an egg, beaten with the blade of a knife to a stiff froth; sprinkle over pounded sugar, and put them into the oven for a minute or two, to dry the egg; dish the pies on a white d'oyley, and serve hot. They may be merely sprinkled with pounded sugar, instead of being glazed. To re-warm them, put the pies on the patty-pans, and let them remain in the oven for 10 minutes or ¼ hour, and they will be almost as good as if freshly made.

TIME: 25 to 30 minutes; 10 minutes to re-warm them.
Average cost; 4*d.* each.
Sufficient, ½ lb. of paste for 4 pies.
Seasonable at Christmas time.

VERY GOOD PUFF PASTE

INGREDIENTS

To every lb. of flour allow 1 lb. butter, and not quite ½ pint water

MODE

Carefully weigh the flour and butter, and have the exact proportion; squeeze the butter well, and afterwards wring it in a clean cloth, that no moisture may remain. Sift the flour, and see that it is perfectly dry. Supposing the quantity to be 1 lb. Of flour, work the whole into a smooth paste, with not quite ½ pint of water, using a knife to mix it with; the proportion of water must be regulated by the discretion of the cook: if too much be added, the paste, when baked, will be tough. Roll it out until it is of an equal thickness of about an inch; break 4 oz. of the butter into small pieces, place these on the paste, sift over it a little flour, fold it over, roll out again, and put another 4 oz. of butter. Repeat the rolling and buttering until the paste has been rolled out 4 times, or equal quantities of flour and butter have been used. Do not omit, every time the paste is rolled out, to dredge a little flour over that and the rolling-pin, to prevent both from sticking. Handle the paste as lightly as possible, and do not press heavily upon it with the rolling-pin. Do not put it into the oven until it is sufficiently hot to raise the paste, for the best prepared paste, if not properly baked, will be good for nothing. Brushing the paste as often as rolled out, and the pieces of butter placed thereon, with the white of an egg assists it to rise in *leaves* or *flakes.*

AVERAGE COST: 1*s.* 8*d.* per lb.

MEDIUM PUFF PASTE

INGREDIENTS

To every lb. of flour allow 8 oz. butter and 3 oz. lard, not quite ½ pint water

MODE

This paste may be made by the directions in the preceding recipe, only using less butter and substituting lard for a portion of it. Mix the flour to a smooth paste with not quite ½ pint of water, then roll it out three times, the first time covering the paste with butter, the second with lard, and the third with butter.

AVERAGE COST: 1*s.* per lb.

MINCEMEAT

INGREDIENTS

2 lbs. raisins
3 lbs. currants
1½ lb. lean beef
3 lbs. beef suet
2 lbs. moist sugar
2 oz. citron
2 oz. candied lemon-peel
2 oz. candied orange-peel
1 small nutmeg
1 pottle* apples
the rind of 2 lemons and the juice of 1
½ pint brandy

MODE

Stone and cut the raisins once or twice across, but do not chop them; wash, dry, and pick the currants free from stalks and grit, and mince the beef and chop the suet very fine; slice the citron and candied peel; grate the nutmeg, and pare, core, and mince the apples; mince the lemon-peel, strain the juice. Mix these ingredients well together, adding the brandy when the other things are well blended; press the whole into a jar, carefully exclude the air, and the mincemeat will be ready for use in a fortnight.

AVERAGE COST FOR THIS QUANTITY: 8*s.*
Seasonable—make this about the beginning of December.

*A small, conical wicker basket.

A PLAIN CHRISTMAS PUDDING FOR CHILDREN

INGREDIENTS

1 lb. flour
1 lb. bread-crumbs
¾ lb. stoned raisins
¾ lb. currants
¾ lb. suet
3 or 4 eggs
milk
2 oz. candied peel
1 teaspoonful powdered allspice
½ saltspoonful salt

MODE

Let the suet be finely chopped, the raisins stoned, and the currants well washed, picked, and dried. Mix these with the other dry ingredients, and stir well together; beat and strain the eggs to the pudding, stir these in, and add just sufficient milk to make it mix properly. Tie it up in a well-floured cloth, put it into boiling water, and boil for at least 5 hours. Serve with a sprig of holly placed in the middle of the pudding, and a little pounded sugar sprinkled over it.

TIME: 5 hours.
Average cost: 1*s.* 9*d.*
Sufficient for 9 or 10 children.
Seasonable at Christmas.

CHRISTMAS PLUM-PUDDING (VERY GOOD)

INGREDIENTS

- 1½ lb. raisins
- ½ lb. currants
- ½ lb. mixed peel
- ¾ lb. bread-crumbs
- ¾ lb. suet
- 8 eggs
- 1 wineglassful brandy

MODE

Stone and cut the raisins in halves, but do not chop them; wash, pick and dry the currants, and mince the suet fine; cut the candied peel into thin slices, and grate down the bread into fine crumbs. When all these dry ingredients are prepared, mix them well together; then moisten the mixture with the eggs, which should be well beaten, and the brandy; stir well, that everything may be very thoroughly blended; and *press* the pudding into a buttered mould; tie it down tightly with a floured cloth, and boil for 5 or 6 hours. It may be boiled in a cloth without a mould, and will require the same time allowed for cooking. As Christmas puddings are usually made a few days before they are required for table, when the pudding is taken out of the pot, hang it up immediately, and put a plate or saucer underneath to catch the water that may drain from it. The day it is to be eaten, plunge it into boiling water, and keep it boiling for at least 2 hours; then turn it out of the mould, and serve with brandy-sauce. On Christmas-day a sprig of holly is usually placed in the middle of the pudding, and about a wineglassful of brandy poured round it, which, at the moment of serving, is lighted, and the pudding thus brought to table encircled in flame.

TIME: 5 or 6 hours the first time of boiling; 2 hours the day it is to be served.

Average cost: 3*s.* 6*d.*

Sufficient for a quart mould, for 7 or 8 persons.

Seasonable on the 25th of December, and on various festive occasions till March.

A Note on the Type

The principal text of this Modern Library edition was set in a digitized version of Janson, a typeface that dates from about 1690 and was cut by Nicholas Kis, a Hungarian working in Amsterdam. The original matrices have survived and are held by the Stempel foundry in Germany. Hermann Zapf redesigned some of the weights and sizes for Stempel, basing his revisions on the original design.

THE MODERN LIBRARY—A LIST OF CURRENT TITLES

The Education of Henry Adams
LOUISA MAY ALCOTT: *Modern Magic*•
DANTE ALIGHIERI: *Inferno; Purgatorio; Paradiso*
SHERWOOD ANDERSON: *Winesburg, Ohio*
RICHARD BURTON, TRANSLATOR: *The Arabian Nights*
ARISTOTLE: *Introduction to Aristotle*
ST. AUGUSTINE: *The City of God*
JANE AUSTEN: *Emma; Mansfield Park; Northanger Abbey; Persuasion; Pride and Prejudice; Sense and Sensibility; The Complete Novels* (Vol. I: *Sense and Sensibility, Pride and Prejudice, Mansfield Park*); (Vol. II: *Emma, Northanger Abbey, Persuasion*)
JAMES BALDWIN: *The Fire Next Time; Go Tell It on the Mountain*
HONORÉ DE BALZAC: *Lost Illusions*
RICHARD BAUSCH: *The Selected Stories*•
MONROE C. BEARDSLEY, EDITOR: *The European Philosophers from Descartes to Nietzsche*•
DANIEL J. BOORSTIN: *The Daniel J. Boorstin Reader*•
ANNE BRONTË: *The Tenant of Wildfell Hall*
CHARLOTTE BRONTË: *Jane Eyre; The Professor; Shirley; Villette*
EMILY BRONTË: *Wuthering Heights*
THOMAS BULFINCH: *Bulfinch's Mythology*
JACOB BURCKHARDT: *The Civilization of the Renaissance in Italy*
EDWIN A. BURTT, EDITOR: *The English Philosophers from Bacon to Mill*•
TRUMAN CAPOTE: *Breakfast at Tiffany's; In Cold Blood; A Christmas Memory, One Christmas, & The Thanksgiving Visitor*
WILLA CATHER: *Death Comes for the Archbishop; My Ántonia*
RAYMOND CHANDLER: *The Big Sleep & Farewell, My Lovely*
GEOFFREY CHAUCER: *The Canterbury Tales*
ANTON CHEKHOV: *Longer Stories from the Last Decade*•
KATE CHOPIN: *The Awakening and Selected Stories*
COLETTE: *My Mother's House & Sido*

•Exclusive to the Modern Library

CONFUCIUS: *The Wisdom of Confucius*
JOSEPH CONRAD: *Nostromo; Youth, Heart of Darkness, Typhoon*
STEPHEN CRANE: *The Red Badge of Courage*
CHARLES DARWIN: *The Origin of Species*
DANIEL DEFOE: *Moll Flanders*
CHARLES DICKENS: *American Notes; A Christmas Carol and Other Stories*•; *Our Mutual Friend; A Tale of Two Cities*
EMILY DICKINSON: *The Selected Poems*
ISAK DINESEN: *Out of Africa; Seven Gothic Tales*
E. L. DOCTOROW: *Ragtime*
JOHN DONNE: *The Complete Poetry and Selected Prose*
FYODOR DOSTOEVSKY: *The Best Short Stories of Dostoevsky; The Brothers Karamazov; Crime and Punishment*
THEODORE DREISER: *Sister Carrie*
W.E.B. DU BOIS: *The Souls of Black Folk*
ALEXANDRE DUMAS: *The Count of Monte Cristo*
ALBERT EINSTEIN: *Ideas and Opinions*
GEORGE ELIOT: *Middlemarch*
RALPH ELLISON: *The Collected Essays*•; *Invisible Man*
RALPH WALDO EMERSON: *Selected Writings*•
FREDERICK EXLEY: *A Fan's Notes*
WILLIAM FAULKNER: *Absalom, Absalom!; Go Down, Moses; Selected Short Stories; Snopes (The Hamlet, The Town, The Mansion)*•; *The Sound and the Fury*
RICHARD FEYNMAN: *The Character of Physical Law*
HENRY FIELDING: *Tom Jones*
F. SCOTT FITZGERALD: *This Side of Paradise*
GUSTAVE FLAUBERT: *Madame Bovary*
SHELBY FOOTE: *The Beleaguered City: The Vicksburg Campaign*•; *Stars in Their Courses: The Gettysburg Campaign*•
E. M. FORSTER: *A Room with a View & Howards End*
SIGMUND FREUD: *The Basic Writings of Sigmund Freud*•; *The Interpretation of Dreams*
EDWARD GIBBON: *The Decline and Fall of the Roman Empire,* Volume I, Volume II, Volume III
JOHANN WOLFGANG VON GOETHE: *The Sorrows of Young Werther* and *Novella*
NIKOLAI GOGOL: *Dead Souls*
GRAHAM GREENE: *The Quiet American*
LORRAINE HANSBERRY: *A Raisin in the Sun*
THOMAS HARDY: *The Collected Novels* (Vol. I: *Far from the Madding Crowd, The Return of the Native, The Mayor of Casterbridge;* Vol. II: *Tess of the d'Urbervilles, Jude the Obscure*); *The Return of the Native*
NATHANIEL HAWTHORNE: *The Complete Novels and Selected Tales* (Vol. I: *Fanshawe, Twice-Told Tales, Mosses from an Old Manse, The Scarlet Letter*)
O. HENRY: *The Best Short Stories*
VICTOR HUGO: *Les Misérables; The Hunchback of Notre-Dame*
JANE JACOBS: *The Death and Life of Great American Cities*

•Exclusive to the Modern Library

HENRY JAMES: *The Wings of the Dove*
WILLIAM JAMES: *The Varieties of Religious Experience*
THOMAS JEFFERSON: *The Life and Selected Writings*
SARAH ORNE JEWETT: *The Country of the Pointed Firs and Other Stories*
JAMES JOYCE: *Dubliners; A Portrait of the Artist as a Young Man; Ulysses*
C. G. JUNG: *The Basic Writings*
FRANZ KAFKA: *Selected Short Stories*
IMMANUEL KANT: *The Philosophy of Kant*
JOHN KEATS: *Complete Poems*
TRACY KIDDER: *The Soul of a New Machine*
LAO-TZU: *Te-Tao Ching*
D. H. LAWRENCE: *Lady Chatterley's Lover; Sons and Lovers*
CLAUDE LÉVI-STRAUSS: *Tristes Tropiques*
A. J. LIEBLING: *Between Meals*•; *The Road Back to Paris*
NORMAN MAILER: *The Executioner's Song*
SIR THOMAS MALORY: *Le Morte d'Arthur*
THOMAS MANN: *Death in Venice & Seven Other Stories; Doctor Faustus; The Magic Mountain*
WILLIAM MAXWELL: *They Came Like Swallows*
CARSON MCCULLERS: *The Heart Is a Lonely Hunter*
HERMAN MELVILLE: *Moby Dick; The Piazza Tales*
JOSEPH MITCHELL: *The Bottom of the Harbor; Joe Gould's Secret*
NANCY MITFORD: *The Pursuit of Love & Love in a Cold Climate*
LADY MURASAKI: *The Tale of Genji*
ALBERT MURRAY: *South to a Very Old Place*
V. S. NAIPAUL: *A Bend in the River*
FRIEDRICH NIETZSCHE: *Basic Writings*•; *Thus Spoke Zarathustra*
FRANK NORRIS: *McTeague*
JOHN O'HARA: *Appointment in Samarra; The Novellas of John O'Hara*•; *A Rage to Live*
EUGENE O'NEILL: *Nine Plays*
DOROTHY PARKER: *The Poetry and Short Stories*
PLATO: *Symposium*
PLUTARCH: *The Lives of the Noble Grecians and Romans* (Volume I, Volume II)
EDGAR ALLAN POE: *The Collected Tales and Poems*
V. S. PRITCHETT: *A Cab at the Door & Midnight Oil*•
MARCEL PROUST: IN SEARCH OF LOST TIME (Vol. I: *Swann's Way;* Vol. II: *Within a Budding Grove;* Vol. III: *The Guermantes Way;* Vol. IV: *Sodom and Gomorrah;* Vol. V: *The Captive & The Fugitive;* Vol. VI: *Time Regained* and *A Guide to Proust*)
JOHN REED: *The Collected Works*•
RAINER MARIA RILKE: *Ahead of All Parting*•
THEODORE ROOSEVELT: *Hunting Trips of a Ranchman & The Wilderness Hunter*•
LILLIAN ROSS: *Picture*
PHILIP ROTH: *Goodbye, Columbus*

•Exclusive to the Modern Library

JAMES SALTER: *A Sport and a Pastime*
SIR WALTER SCOTT: *Ivanhoe*
WILLIAM SHAKESPEARE: *The Comedies; The Histories and Poems; The Tragedies*
MARY SHELLEY: *Frankenstein*
PERCY BYSSHE SHELLEY: *Complete Poems*
ADAM SMITH: *The Wealth of Nations*
ALEXANDER SOLZHENITSYN: *Cancer Ward*
GERTRUDE STEIN: *The Autobiography of Alice B. Toklas*
STENDHAL: *The Red and the Black*
LAURENCE STERNE: *Tristram Shandy & A Sentimental Journey*
BRAM STOKER: *Dracula*
HARRIET BEECHER STOWE: *Uncle Tom's Cabin*
WILLIAM STYRON: *The Confessions of Nat Turner*
JONATHAN SWIFT: *Gulliver's Travels*
PETER TAYLOR: *The Old Forest and Other Stories*
HUNTER S. THOMPSON: *Fear and Loathing in Las Vegas and Other American Stories*•
HENRY DAVID THOREAU: *Walden and Other Writings*
JAMES THURBER: *The Thurber Carnival*
LEO TOLSTOY: *Anna Karenina; War and Peace*
JEAN TOOMER: *Cane*
ANTHONY TROLLOPE: *The Way We Live Now*
MARK TWAIN *The Adventures of Huckleberry Finn; Life on the Mississippi*
GORE VIDAL: *Lincoln*
VOLTAIRE: *Candide and Philosophical Letters*

•Exclusive to the Modern Library

PHYLLIS CERF WAGNER AND HERBERT WISE, EDITORS: *Great Tales of Terror and the Supernatural*
IZAAK WALTON AND CHARLES COTTON: *The Compleat Angler*
H. G. WELLS: *The Island of Dr. Moreau*
EUDORA WELTY: *Selected Stories*
WALT WHITMAN: *Leaves of Grass*
OSCAR WILDE: *The Picture of Dorian Gray*
EDMUND WILSON: *Axel's Castle*
WILLIAM BUTLER YEATS, EDITOR: *Irish Fairy and Folktales*
MARGUERITE YOURCENAR: *Memoirs of Hadrian*

Modern Library Audios

THOMAS BULFINCH: *Bulfinch's Mythology*
STEPHEN CRANE: *The Red Badge of Courage*
SHELBY FOOTE: *The Beleaguered City: The Vicksburg Campaign; Stars in Their Courses: The Gettysburg Campaign*
EDGAR ALLAN POE: *Selected Tales and Poems*
OSCAR WILDE: *The Picture of Dorian Gray*

The Modern Library/BBC AudioBooks

WILLIAM SHAKESPEARE: *Hamlet; King Lear; Macbeth; Othello*

The Book of Genesis
The New Testament
Psalms and Proverbs